The work before you is purely fictional. Any resemblance to real persons (living or dead), corporations, or other restaurants is coincidental.

For all the hard workers out there

For my children and my wife

For you, the reader

I. Shift Meeting

Every shift meeting there are two people still drunk from the previous night, six servers that are severely hungover, and one that is missing. The meeting commences at 10:30 am as energy drinks and coffee are inhaled by the pint. The restaurant smells like cleaning supplies and fresh water for a while. The ventilation system carries the scent of various spices and meats throughout the entire restaurant. It's never too greasy in the kitchen and the odor is inviting to those who can stomach this particular aroma. To some of the workers it's like walking into the home they never had. Just like one of their mottos and slogans, "home cooking away from home...at its finest."

Despite everyone having the same schedule, the servers never arrive at the same time. Some arrive 10 minutes early for their shift, and some arrive 10 minutes late. Gez always arrives late and Ronald always arrives early. Jordan would tease him except that Jordan is missing from the meeting. Most of the staff have a high respect for him because he works there by choice and not out of necessity. Some will joke and say that he doesn't have a life. To which he'll say, like he always does without hesitation and with purpose, "I don't have a life; that's why I'm here. That's why I'm rotting away with you."

Once the drinks, greetings, and love are shared by the POS (that's point of sale for some of the uninitiated) and everybody is clocked in, they sit in the back dining area that is meant for large parties and groups. The servers sit in all of the tables and the girls rest their feet on the booths that were cleaned and sanitized just the night before. They sit with friends, or rather people they can actually relate to. *Cliques.* They all have cliques.

This weekend, the workers will be overworked and underpaid because they are short staffed, there is a nervousness in knowing what is going to happen once business picks up. The first three hours are a joke and servers hate their shifts because they can barely make a bill during their work hours. Chandler's Casual Eatery doesn't have a patio section so all of the servers work inside. Sometimes, they don't get seated until one hour into their designated shift. One hour of standing around with no pay, eagerly waiting to serve, and anticipating disappointment. Around 1 pm, after the "normal" people run their morning errands and are famished, they come in, one group after another. It keeps going on until closing time. Alden, the general manager, likes to be the MOD (manager on duty) during these busy weekends. He likes to oversee the business operations to ensure everything runs smoothly under his reign. He anticipates the business day and mentally prepares himself before coaching the staff as they trickle in. He puts out his cigarette and takes one last sip of his coffee before speaking.

Dante is working on the seating chart. Alden looks around at all the faces he leads and asks, "Everyone here?"

With red eyes and a slightly scared intonation, Dante explains,

"No. Jordan is late."

"Fuckin' Jordan. Piece of shit."

The general manager hails from Brooklyn, New York, and wears gaudy jewelry. His accent is regionally thick and his language is coarse and tough but only because he skips right to the point. Blunt. Very blunt.

"I think I'm paranoid," he begins. He is calm at first with his hand over his mouth looking around at each of his employees. He examines and judges them for shit they haven't even done yet. He can look in their eyes and predict the trouble they will bring him when the restaurant is in the weeds.

"I must be *fuckin'* paranoid! I just keep thinking that we're not getting our shit together. That we're not doing our very best. People are talkin' out there. I go up to tables, and I greet everyone that I can, but when I hear

shit like you're *giving away food* that should be paid for...
for what? What good is that doing anyone? You're
gonna get the fuckin' tip you deserve. *Jesus!* Why are
you giving away food for a shitty fuckin' *two dollar tip?*
Are you outta your *fucking* mind?"

The employees sit and listen. Some are attentive
while others are checking for any new developments in
their social life on their phones. The staff comes together
every Saturday morning to listen to one of these rants. It
was the same as it was last week.

"Don't get me wrong, my mantra has always been that
service is king, but we can't be giving away food. If I
catch you doing that shit I will tell you to *get outta my
restaurant.* That shit can't be going on. It's costing *us*
money and it's costing *you* money. Higher bills, higher
tips; so what if someone is gonna give you ten percent?
Ten percent of fifty dollars is a lot higher than ten
percent of twenty. You upsell. You have add-ons.
There's a reason this book is on the table."

He grabs a small booklet with leather binding and the
restaurant logo on the front. Within the pages of this
book contains the key to more money for the servers
and the restaurant. It features the best photographs of
the products Chandler's offers. Unbeknownst to the
customers, in order to get these pictures, the food is
often fake, or made with various ingredients to make the

product more appealing. Like commercials on TV and ads everywhere, it's all for effect.

"You think it's just there to look *cute?* You think it's just there for a child to draw on? This is a TOOL you use to sell! You're a salesman!"

He slams the book on the closest table. His face is red. His voice is getting stronger and stronger.

" *You're* customer service, you're the king of your station, of your section and Service is king! Service is king! We do legendary service here! How many times do I have to tell you before you understand? I see this week after week and quite frankly I'm tired of telling you. I'm gonna start doing follows on you all. I'm gonna talk to every fuckin' table that comes in here. I'm going to make sure you're doing everything that you are supposed to be doing. I'm gonna weed all you dumb fucks out of here faster than any of you can greet a table. I have stacks of applications and résumés of people that want to come in here and work. *Actually work.* Not sit around, complain and ask what you're doing with your life."

Alden contemplates the meaning of life while giving this speech. He puts his hand to his face and rubs his beard that only grows during wintertime. His tone changes with more enthusiasm.

"Let's thank Ronald over here for doing such an amazing job. I always count on him for picking up your slack; he's here for a reason. You're all here for a reason. Whether it's to pay for school, make some extra cash, get some extra commission, pay for that wedding ring, you're here for a reason. To make money. I'm here to make money. We want a win-win-win situation. If the customer is happy, they give you money. I'm happy, we make money. You're happy, you go home with money."

He calls out servers individually.

"Ronald what are you here for?"

"I'm here to make money."

"Money for what?"

"Well, I'm helping my wife finish her school. I'm working more so she can have more time to finish school."

"Chelsea what are you here for?"

Chelsea is a bit nervous and shy. Not too shy for the job at hand, but Alden scares the hell out of her sometimes.

"Um, I'm here because I have to pay rent."

"So it's your livelihood. That's okay. You need this job, and this job needs you! You make the customer happy with excellent service, they tip you a large amount of money, you win, we have a returning guest, and the restaurant wins. Three wins."

He paces down the walkway between the tables and addresses the staff.

"You can make that happen with every customer—you just have to buy into the idea that *service* is king! We give legendary service! I don't make shit up. It's proven. It's there for a reason. Service is king, so go out there and make it happen. You can get by with a bad kitchen and great service. But you can't get by with horrible service and a great kitchen. Remember that. I've seen it destroy places. For god's sake, smile more! Go the extra mile. Do I need to retrain you? I shouldn't, and I don't want to. I don't have that energy. Get out there and let's bust our asses today. We have a lot of doubles so I'll make sure you get some time to eat. The rest of you are staying until the dinner crowd gets here. Do your best, and make lots of money."

The staff remains quiet for 20 seconds before moving. The staff in the front is no more enthused or awake than they were when they arrived. They're just sitting there waiting for their commands.

"Alright, let's get to work."

When they scatter, some of the out-of-touch workers are confused as the hangovers still throb through their heads. Before their hangover can beat again, a party of 14 is ready to eat.

"Keep yourselves focused today. No distractions. Let's give the best service."

Alden reassures his staff like a little league coach with nothing to say when they are down by 40 points with two minutes left to play. He knows they have lost, but they have to finish the game anyway.

Most managers despise what they do. They find it despicable. But this particular man is a twisted individual. Only a masochist and a sadist would do his job, and do it with the tastefulness he does. He thrives for a challenge.

II. Rolling: Silverware

The employees work to survive. When it's busy, the servers will do their best not to sacrifice their skills, but on some busy occasions the line will fail, the staff will be short, and the patrons will complain about cold and undercooked food.

Isabel was running her mind as fast as her legs. Could she remember everything that everyone wanted? In such a high-volume restaurant, if a server even looks the wrong way, they could be behind for hours. Could she remember to refill the sodas and teas on Table 44, while making a salad for Table 45, and then put in an order for Table 46 while not forgetting about the extra ranch for Table 42? Or was it 43?

She was losing her mind and didn't want to go back to check, so instead she made sure to get extra items, condiments and drinks that she didn't need. She yelled for her ticket times just before she left the kitchen area. Once she dropped her items off to each table she took responsibility and was completely honest to all her guests as to why their food and service was taking such a long time.

"Hello sir, ma'am, sorry about the wait, we are short staffed today, but no need to worry, I'll make sure your food comes out soon and please do not hesitate to call me. My manager's name is Meredith. She will be more than happy to accommodate your needs if you see her."

The customers were pleasant and understanding but when it's that busy, it's easy for a table to get heated. The end never seems to come soon enough but the light at the end of the tunnel was near. Isabel was able to explain all that went on behind the scenes and earned some trust in their short-lived relationship during dinnertime.

Finally able to catch up, she now begins her nightly side work duties that were assigned at the beginning of the shift. Tonight she'll be responsible for sanitizing the drink station and after this task is done, once her tables leave, she will have to clean and sweep. After that, she'll finally get to sit down and count her earnings for the evening. To be able to leave she'll need to get the sign off from Meredith or Dante but only after she and her workers roll all the freshly cleaned silverware from the dish pit.

The restaurant wants people who are willing to get paid next to nothing while working for tips only. If a person is willing to work hard for low check amounts, Chandler's will not fail to pass on this exploitation.

If a person can bus a table and work for less than minimum wage and tip share then they'll be hired.

If a person can add, subtract, put up with emotional and sometimes physical and sexual abuse from management, other employees, cooks and creepy ass guests then they'll be hired.

Fucking hired.

It doesn't matter where a person comes from or where the person is going; what matters is if they show up for their scheduled shift.

The day of long wait times, ticket times, and a never-ending herd of people is finally over. The busy shift brought surprises, but everyone was focused on getting through it rather than hating on each other and talking shit like children. The staff was surprised how smooth it all went because sometimes, their egos can get the better of them. No yelling, fighting, or screaming, just the workers there to do the tasks at hand with Jordan doing the best job at motivating each of them.

Jordan wanted all the money to spend on his weekly big after shift party he hosts. Tonight, word around the soda fountain is that everyone is invited. All were going except for a few servers that didn't quite fit the mold. It wasn't that they didn't enjoy a good time; they just had better things to do.

The servers are ecstatic to take home their earnings for a relatively smooth shift. Everything for once is good in the industry except for Isabel. Isabel is a skinny young Hispanic girl, about 5'2" and 119 pounds. Incredibly petite and looks as if she could easily be broken in half by a swift wind, a small bump, or an obnoxious attitude. Her glasses frame her face as if she bought them when she was 20 pounds heavier because she struggles to keep them lined to her brown eyes. Her hair, tangled and messy, is full of kitchen grease and some random sauce. She thinks it's honey mustard, but she's not sure and isn't going to taste it. Once the dust settles and she's done sweeping from the wild night, she sits down to count her money and the panic sinks in.

Her book is missing. Her lifeline to the restaurant, complete with all of the customer's payments, credit card slips, and cash is gone. Sadly, for Isabel this was a good night. Finally she had enough to pay for that haircut she needed. She could've enjoyed a nice dinner too or give that extra cash to her little sister for her upcoming birthday. But it's gone. All of it. Gone. Nothing to take home and nothing to give Chandler's. For every cash transaction Isabel receives, she is required to hold onto it until the end of the night. The servers keep all the credit card slips from the night along with all of the cash. If the server receives nothing but credit card tips and tip slips, they hang on to that, then hand it to the MOD at the end of the shift. Chandler's pays them the amount they made based on what's on the slips. If a server makes nothing but cash payments, the servers owe what the computer says they sold from the restaurant and keep the change. So what happens when someone loses everything like Isabel does?

She'll be lucky if she still has a job. Isabel made $50 in tip slips that she won't get to see because she has no proof that she was tipped. As for the cash she owes, according to the computer's tracking information, she will have to pay that out of her own pocket. What a shame, really because she owes the restaurant $145 out of her own pocket.

One hundred forty-five fucking dollars.

In rare instances, managers like Alden and Charlie have the authority to void checks and tables that paid cash as if they were never there. This means that all of the cash that was lost cancels out and she's only left to pay out tip share.

Charlie and Alden are not working now.

Dante and Meredith, the lower level managers, however, do not have the authority to do this. Not that someone like Dante would anyway as he is the type to squeeze every inch of life out of their poor little servers. Suffocating them with his aggression, language, and dirty looks.

Sorry. She'll have to pay.

One hundred forty-five fucking dollars.

She begins to tear up but tries to hide it. She can't. She moves out and sits at a table that Daniel is cleaning up and he just happens to be in the right place at the wrong time. He sees her and decides to involve himself. Perhaps he thinks it will win him some type of molten lava cake points. With his heart of gold, and with the ridiculous amount of money he made, he decides to donate $20 to the Isabel fund. He understands what it means to fall short because he'd been there when he first started working. He wished someone had done the same for him. He walks around and asks everyone to see if they can donate. Chelsea, Meredith, Stephanie, Gez, Jordan, Natalie, and anyone else who has the money to spare. A lot of servers have lost money, but several don't lose their pride while doing it. Daniel ends up collecting $165 and surprises her with the money and even tells her to keep the extra $20. What a wonderful person he is!

Wonderful indeed to go out of his way to fix another person's problem.

The pain of losing cash happens to everyone and due to the high volume of tables, there happens to be a surplus of great intentions and money to show for it. It's a rite of passage as a server because even the most experienced struggle to hold on to hundreds of dollars a night. Daniel gives the money to Isabel and she pays off Dante. She's upset she won't be going home with her full earnings, but she knows she'll see the difference on her check.

Isabel thanks Daniel as her tears clear up and she joins the staff as they finish closing and cleaning the restaurant. He accepts it, but slightly disappointed that it wasn't followed with any kind of physical thanks. Not a big deal to him as he continues with his side work. It's dirty. Hot chocolate sauce everywhere, ice thrown on the floors, cups scattered throughout the serving station, and ranch on every part of their bodies. There is gravy on the ceiling in the dish pit from when Jordan threw a piece of fried chicken out of frustration. All of this grit and dirt needs to be cleaned up before they all leave. All of it must be spotless. The floor needs cleaning, the line needs cleaning, ice stocked, glasses stocked, sauces refilled, floors swept and vacuumed, salt and pepper filled up, ketchup bottles filled, and of course the silverware needs to be rolled up for use tomorrow. Hundreds and maybe thousands of forks and knives need to be wrapped up tight in napkins so they can be ripped out and used again and again and again. Hopefully, the forks and knives are clean enough to sort.

Servers typically get a set count to roll at the beginning of the shift, but now they must do as much as they can so that the Sunday church crowd will be ready to make it through their lunch. Daniel and Isabel begin to separate the knives, spoons, and forks to make it easier for the rest.

"Were you able to bring home anything after all?" Daniel begins.

"Twenty dollars. It could be worse, I guess."

"It could be a lot worse."

They are awkwardly silent. Isabel would of course be in a much better mood had she not lost her book. Shame. She wonders what happened. Did a guest steal it? A busser? Another server? It couldn't have been another server; there is a code that servers never steal from one another. At least, so she *thought*, but the greed of people continued to surprise her throughout her start as a waitress. Chandler's breeds the type of horrible people out in the world. Usually, new servers and employees start off very innocent and happy, but when working in the industry, it's just a matter of time before they transform into something and someone else entirely. She's pretty good at keeping a smile on her face and she tries to forget about her problem, but it continues to swell up inside more and more. She was never good at controlling her emotions when she's upset. Her mind would always tell her to soak in the pain, but she never could.

In her head is a battle that she is losing and losing bad. Her panic controls her. Something that will always stay with her, deep down and inside herself. She's screaming to let go, but the restaurant won't let go of her. Now all this built-up pressure is exploding like an angry cook being yelled at by Alden. She lets it go like she has so many times before this.

"I don't think I've ever heard you speak like that."

"It's bullshit!" she screams. "I came in and worked my ass off. All day. All fuckin' day. All day. Twelve hours. More than that. It's all gone. My whole day. Who does that?"

The servers gather together as customers do, sitting across from one another in their chairs waiting for something to entertain them. Finally, after a dramatically long three minutes of sitting in silence, hundreds of forks, knives, and napkins appear in front of them waiting to be rolled tightly in a basket to give back to the dirty hands of the customers. Really, people eat off of one another every single day and just don't realize it. The world inside a restaurant is a shared one, and washing the plates and hands isn't enough to cleanse the dirt every person carries: it's something that can never be rid of, so it's easier to accept it than to change it.

Daniel and Isabel sit and roll. Chelsea joins in as well. They begin to take on fork after fork with their hands cramping after they are a quarter of the way done. It never ends, and yet they still race to finish the task even though they aren't going anywhere. They think they are free, but tomorrow morning they will all be back for more.

Chelsea's voice is strained, barely loud enough because she's been screaming all day. She's not known for being a talker and a socialite, but this weekend deserves her words.

"You got your book stolen tonight? I feel like the restaurant steals from me every night. I made a lot of money today, but I had to give $50 in tip share? That's ridiculous. You should be blaming *them* for making you pay. Otherwise, they should've been able to take care of you. Isn't that what a job is supposed to do?"

"Not this job. Someone stole from me. I just don't know who."

"It's okay. Everyone is stealing from everyone these days."

"You're Chelsea, right?"

"Yes."

"We don't really talk much."

Chelsea doesn't really talk to anyone. It's not that she is completely closed off, but she feels that she can't really relate to any of her coworkers. Oftentimes, she thinks that she is unique and special to the world. If she were to only open her mouth, she would see that her viewpoints on life match those of her coworkers.

"Well, I don't really talk to anyone much."

"How long have you been here?"

"Why does everyone ask me that?"

"What do you mean?"

Chelsea squints in disbelief—like she doesn't understand. Isabel is caught off guard and surprised that she is actually engaged in a conversation with her. Really, that she is engaged in a conversation that doesn't involve the common subjects of a typical Chandler's server.

"Just...every conversation here starts with the same thing: how long have you been here, how much did you make, last night I got so wasted I was shwasted. I had a wet dream about you, get a drink with me, let's go to my place. *Every* time someone tries to talk to me...but don't worry about it hun, I didn't mean anything by it. Just an observation."

Isabel is a bit confused and distracted from her night's losses. She doesn't seem to understand why Chelsea talks the way she does, but goes with it and doesn't stop her. They continue to pile the rolled up silverware into an unsanitized plastic bus bin.

"Oh." she responds with an awkward blink.

Chelsea continues. "I've been here for five years. Just a job. I wish I could change it, but you know I have to take care of the kids and pay for school."

"You're in school?"

"No. I'm already done with school. Graduated about three years ago."

Daniel chimes in and asks Chelsea, "What, in art?"

"Well... yes actually."

"Is that why you're still here?" asks Isabel.

"A job is a job. I didn't get a stupid degree like art history or feminist studies. I got a degree in Digital Communication Arts. You know. Adobe stuff. Photoshop, InDesign, Illustrator. I do freelance stuff right now."

"You?" Daniel is shocked to find out that Chelsea possesses knowledge in digital media. His preconceived notion of her fails him, as it does in most instances.

"Yes, me. Freelance. I know how to use a computer a lot better than you sucker!"

"What do you work on?" asks Isabel.

"I work on everything." continues Chelsea, wrapping the napkin tight around her eightieth roll. "I do book covers, websites, logos, anything. This job is to help pay off that stupid high dollar college debt. Once I get enough, I'm leaving this nonsensical job."

Isabel chimes in. "I can't wait until I leave. I had to take this job because I wanted to move out. I couldn't stand living with my mom and dad. Those two are insane. I finally got my own place with a friend, except she's high all the time and I'm stuck in a lease. Except, because of that exact reason, my mom and dad will never come over."

"Why not, too religious?" responds Chelsea.

"Oh them? Hard core. They are into the church like crazy. They spent more time at church and not any time on me. I'd be alone on Sundays after mass. They donate all of their time to the needy, but drink like fish, and never did anything with me. I guess church was something to make them feel better about themselves."

Daniel listens intently. He thinks church would be a good thing for his family, but is also terrified for the judgment he may receive. It appeals to him because he feels he may get to be a part of something. He wishes his parents understood God, but instead they don't have the time for Him or any moral obligation for that matter. He doesn't add any substance to the conversation because it's a subject he doesn't know much about, but instead observes the tension adding up. He gets up, runs to the hostess stand to get more napkins for the group. He pauses and looks at the door. It's so dark out there that you can't see the benches and plants in front of the restaurant. It's quiet, unlike it was hours ago. He notices the music for the first time playing above in the speakers. He's not sure who the female singer is. Perhaps Pink, or maybe Katy Perry? He was never interested in pop songs, but stopped to focus on the vocals and the rhythm. Maybe this was something he was missing out on. Maybe he can change his way of thinking, the way he changed his mind about pop music.

Chelsea doesn't believe in institutionalized religion. She believes that people who go to church are liars and hypocrites. Her experience with church was full of speculation because most of the people who were "in power" had no idea what they were actually talking about, as most people in power don't. She goes on: "I don't like church. I believe in God. I love the ideas behind the Bible. Most of the time people misquote it though, and all to fit their own agendas. I grew up around people like that. I always wanted to know more about faith in general. Nobody knew how to give me an answer. Like, I wanted to know how this all tied in with the science I was learning in school. Or for historical evidence, and nobody ever gave me a straight answer. I had to go finding my own. I guess I still am."

Isabel begins to look at Chelsea differently than before. She wants to know more and asks her more personal questions.

"You don't have to answer, but do you teach your kids about it?"

"I do. I tell them about it, but I let them make up their own minds. I'm not going to beat them or kick them out if they don't agree with me."

"How noble of you," Daniel says in a scoff.

"Now if they get caught doing something they're not supposed to be doing I'm going to beat their asses!" The three of them laugh. They slow down in rolling and indulge each other in jokes and anecdotes. Each one of them is learning something new about the other. Daniel starts to speak out a bit more and comes out of his own shell.

"I can't believe this stuff. Today, I had a table. Full of Mexicans. They were making fun of me the entire time. I did everything I could and they didn't leave me shit. They practically stiffed me."

"That's Mexicans for you." says Isabel.

"I'm Mexican." says Daniel.

"That's funny."

"I'm being serious."

"No you're not."

"I'm dead serious."

"No you're not."

"Like I said, they were making fun of me. They thought I couldn't understand them. They were no older than 21. They kept talking shit. I know I look white, but I'm totally fluent in Spanish. Both of my parents are Mexican. My dad grew up in a small town, and my mom's family was from Mexico. Shit, my dad's first language was Spanish! Just because I look white doesn't mean anything."

"Dude," says Chelsea, "I thought you were Korean." They explode in laughter. The silverware doesn't seem to exist anymore. They fill up a couple baskets of silverware and stop. It's sour that they have to leave when barely getting to know one another. Chelsea goes home to her two kids to relieve her mother from watching them and Isabel goes home to a pothead she finds amusing, another girl that keeps her baked for days like this.

"I better hurry up and get out of here." Chelsea gathers her things and removes her apron. She uncovers her silhouette of a thick and proportionate body. Her nimble, frail fingers sharpen the edges of her stainless apron into a perfect square. Why was her apron so clean compared to her coworkers? Does she not work as hard? Does she not do as much as the next person does? Is she even capable of this job and can she keep up with life outside of this restaurant? She ponders all of this as she enters the last four digits of her social security number in the POS to clock out.

Daniel packs up the baskets on top of one another to carry to the front of the hostess stand. "Well y'all, it has been real, it has been fun. And it's been a fuckin' nightmare all in one. Have a good night."

The girls part ways with one another, but just as Isabel leaves Daniel stops her.

"Hey. I know you had a bad night. I'm sorry. Here. I made a lot of money tonight and had a lucky table."

Daniel handed her $40.

"Oh no, you don't have to do this. Please don't."

"No it's okay I made a lot. Plus I'm just going to blow it on booze. I'm okay. Take it."

Isabel sighs and smiles like she finally got a break. She accepts his gift and finds out that within the crazy walls kept up by the greedy and gluttonous, she can still find hope and good people.

III. MOD: Meredith On Duty

Meredith is sitting in the manager's office. It's a small room that's no larger than a fancy woman's walk-in closet. Somehow the room fits three people, a computer, and a desk. She is waiting for her staff to finish their nightly side work. Her hand is resting on her forehead as she sips on a sweet ice tea. On days like today, as busy as it was, she begs to question herself. Why here? Why *this* industry? Why doesn't she look for another job? Why the fuck is she still putting up with it the banality of saving adults from throwing temper tantrums? All over a meal.

Meredith just began her 10th year in the service industry. When she started she had dreams and ambitions that she forgot about when she was promoted to a shift supervisor. Once there, a young 21 year old took the money instead of... something else... something that she can't quite remember. She doesn't enjoy her job per se, but does enjoy getting close with her workers. She enjoys a drink after work on Saturdays and never posts anything on Facebook because it would be deemed unprofessional. Her life looks much better online. Her mind is constantly rambling about her surroundings, and she has a very hard time keeping out of her head. She lets out a long sigh as she's nearing the end of her day.

She says the same thing every time she counts the money from the servers. She says it like a prayer.

"God, how do I do this. Keep me going just for another day."

Not everyone understands the industry and Meredith believes it's a spiritual thing. She's always there and firmly believes that everyone should be required to wait tables in order to graduate high school so they can understand what hard work means and perhaps gain some more empathy towards each other. She knows how fake the place can be. How fake the guests are, and how fake the servers are with each other. There's not an actual home cooked meal here. Not great, anyway. Not even at Chandler's the amazing casual eatery.

Just before her shift, she waits by her car. There is a parking lot that sits right above a small creek. It constantly smells like raw shit, and yet, without that smell, Meredith doesn't think she'd be able to properly go about her day. The creek is mostly dry and naked from the Texas heat, exposing the rocks, grass, animals, and litter. Beer cans and cigarette butts. Surprising to all, a dead body never appeared below. Meredith likes to fantasize about that. One day, Jordan, or maybe her manager, Alden, would be found dead by stab wounds, or a gunshot to the face. Perhaps the body would be too distorted to identify by traditional methods. Then the restaurant would shut down and she would be free. There are other ways to break the chains of a job, but none as fun and fulfilling. She would be the one to find the body sitting in decay. Taken out by someone who snapped.

Meredith's life isn't that exciting though. Twenty feet above the bottom of this creek and today the water is only two feet deep. It's comical that the restaurant was built on this lot right before the highway started construction. The construction of the highway has detoured any type of business they once received. *What a waste of money,* she thinks. Her management and corporate guys tell her that once the construction ends, they will be producing so much profit that everyone will be making bank. There is no hurry to complete the project. Either way, she can't complain about the view that sits in front of her now. It's a nice sight to see. Water. Flowing life in front of her...and how the trash of her workers disrupt it.

Meredith pours her soul and all her reasons to live into this restaurant. She works about 50 to 70 hours a week, with one day off per week. She doesn't sleep and has no time for her new fiancé or herself. Every day she gets trapped in the web of drama her other workers spin. Drama that includes guest complaints, kitchen complaints, and even personal complaints. It's something she hears all day every day. It's at this point that she becomes numb to what's around her. She's looked at like the mother of the workers, being there for them all, listening, helping each employee grow. It's her restaurant, her home. She knows everything that happens, from all the drinks stolen to all the hearts broken, as if it's her sole purpose here. Her real purpose is to get a paycheck to pay for that expensive wedding she doesn't want and that big house that she does. Maybe she could go into counseling and put those empathetic skills to use that she uses on her patrons and coworkers. Instead, she'll buy shoes she'll never wear, outfits she may put on once, and other shit like synthesizers she'll never play. Maybe one day she'll get to start that all-girl new wave band.

When interviewing for management, the one question that was repeatedly asked to her is whether she can handle the operational duties and the responsibility because "it takes a certain kind of crazy." Someone crazy like Meredith who loves the money and the busy atmosphere. She is the kind of crazy that will thrive. The job's havoc, the day to day occurrences come from nothing; unimaginable disorder created by starving guests. What occurs is simply the consequence of one action and one choice. It is a constant tidal wave of emotional destruction.

Meredith puts up with it because she needs to and because she's fucking good at it. She endures mindless tasks, internal pain, and complete trauma from both her workers and her guests but to her, the cost of giving others the best dining experience means much more than money and servers don't understand the true pride. She works hard and cares enough to place that delicious hot plate of food in front of the guest.

It can be unbelievable; the multiple lives that come in to eat here and the others that come to work. The patrons of the restaurant world, and the consumers, buy into this mindset that anyone can trick themselves into being important.

Meredith laments in the passing days as the cooks on the line are ready to plate food while servers are yelling at the top of their lungs for a condiment and their orders.

"Where's my fuckin' ranch!"

"I need this chicken on the fly!" another will scream.

"My shit is fucking raw!"

Observe and fix. That's her job. Like a mother. She doesn't have any kids of her own but she does see her staff as her own "children."

Through the eyes of Meredith when any of her employees is putting forth as much effort as she is, this *means everything*. Even though it is not what they all love to do, they are still working towards a specific goal: to get these asshole customers out the fucking door so they can go get drunk.

It wasn't always as bad as it is now at Chandler's. There are horrible influences and practices at other locations, and of all the places she has worked, Chandler's seems to carry the worst turnover and leadership of them all no matter what changes are made. Now she is a part of the system that she once declared to take down. She does her best to keep everyone content and it works well when everyone is treated with mutual respect but recently that's not the case. The staff is hardly happy and when they try to hide it Meredith can see right through their façade. This is what separates her from the rest of her management team. She is a safe haven for the horrible things that happen. The staff—"her kids"— provide an even deeper purpose than just getting her paycheck.

The business is an abusive relationship and her job is constantly beating her down, hard, and good, but it takes care of her basic needs when she needs it. She holds on to her job in a way that most people wouldn't attempt.

Meredith longs for the carelessness she sees in each of her staff. She envies their abilities to escape reality and partake in illicit substances to endure the abusive and back breaking work that she does so often.

Her staffers make money to drink and get high because they want to forget the day. They don't want to remember that people are going to tip like shit while treating them like scum.

Most of the servers that work for Meredith are aware that the table sitting down in front of them already know what they are going to tip. It's a stereotype and an assumption like most things that happen here at Chandler's. No matter how good or bad the service is the tip is predetermined. The only real people that tip are those that have shared the battle ground with the staff. The regulars make it worth it. They keep Meredith grounded with their philosophical one liners and their high tabs and drinks they buy her after the shift is over. A lot of servers here, like a lot of the places that Meredith worked in the past, can't last long enough to get their own regulars.

They are the smart ones.

It's sad to see them go, but to Meredith, it's even sadder to see them stay. She's seen a young kid out of school with so much ambition, and so much profound idealism and optimism, just fall apart. When sex, drugs and alcohol are available, it's easy to abandon the dream. It's easier to do this than to change. Some make it out, but others let the substance get the best of them.

Meredith begins to write down her shift summary for the manager's log. As she traces a doodle on a notepad she remembers a girl, so beautiful like a model, with a classic look. Her name was Diana. *Was she 18? 19? Couldn't have been older than 19...*At the time the young girl had dark hair and bright blue eyes that were calming to the soul. She started working in the summer as a hostess but once she was exposed to the lifestyles of those around her, she didn't last long. It's a shame what happened to her and yet Meredith has seen it happen every day the same way.

Meredith types away on her report. *Isabel lost her server book today and claims it was stolen by a guest or another employee. Nobody knew what happened and all denied the act of theft.*

After the shift is over, the servers go out and observe their versions of church to celebrate reaping the fruits of their labor. Their jobs make them too busy for God. Just before the workers head off, some of her servers and staff will disappear to the dry storage, the restroom, and the walk-in to trade information, details, and *other* paraphernalia...nothing too damaging.

The people that indulge in heavy use don't typically last that long in the restaurant industry... or any other job, really. Meredith notices the workers are up to no good when the restaurant is still left in a poor and dirty condition. Still, like a loyal hooker taking care of her pimp, she'll do what needs to be done for the betterment of Chandler's. She knows what they're doing but just focuses on getting through the shift.

Throughout the shift, her "kids" will reassure each other that they will make it out after it's all over. It seems that they do it to validate themselves and invite everyone who can go—everyone they *want* to go. They always invite Meredith to go out but she'll use her fiancé as an excuse to skip the party.

Jordan had the bright idea to invite the minors to come and play. That's a party killer for some of the older servers and bartenders, but not for Jordan; this is something that he thrives on. With him and Dante, they can cause a lot of damage to someone's life. They don't seem to be picky anymore. There is no prejudice amongst themselves but only on the customers.

Meredith decides at the last minute if she'll go see Jordan or if she'll just go home. At this point, as she's just checked out another server to leave, she'll justify it to herself.

"I have to look after my kids. Can't have anything go wrong under my watch."

There's another reason she'll go out. It's something inside her that's telling her she doesn't want to be held back from doing what she wants. Maybe it's a feeling of

37

being trapped in her relationship, or being trapped in general. She's got this certain desperation in her voice and eyes. She doesn't spill her guts to anyone. And no matter how many hours she works or watches her employees work, at the end of the week, they are always out and doing something they shouldn't be. They could work all day, running on fumes, and with not a thing to eat, but yet, there they go into the night to spend what little energy they have with each other.

Meredith will be there to bring the food left over from the shift, or drinks to get her staff by. She can't have them starve and she'll feed them when she can. At times, a good story could come out of these gatherings, but usually with Meredith being mother to them, things are uneventful. Her "kids" think they are funnier than what they seem, so their stories out of context are horrible and boring. She won't correct any of them and will just provide her ear to listen when they need.

She really shouldn't be going out with them, or hanging out with them off hours, as it could get her in trouble with the higher ups, but then again—who's keeping tabs? As management, she should be making responsible decisions but she's still a girl in a woman's body. She started as one of them so why should her hours or the title make social life unenjoyable? She'll have her small moments of rebellion that will just shake her chains but won't do enough to break them. Who knows when the day will come when she gets the courage to be what she wants to be.

Off to Jordan's.

One by one they all leave. Meredith will take the cash of the servers and make sure all of their tables are spotless. She'll check off each of her "kids" and ensure they listened to her and did their chores. She'll inspect the drink station, the dessert station, the salad bar. She'll make sure the expo line is clear from any specs of sauce, and the floors have been swept and mopped. The dressings and condiments will have to be full, and if they're not she'll send the server back to do it again and do it right.

"Do it right the first time and you won't have to do it again," she'll say to Jordan, and he'll hurriedly run off to the walk-in to refill his sauces. She'll make sure the grill is clean, and the walls and dish pit are complete and clear of any dirty dishes and silverware. Usually the dishwasher is the last one to leave as the servers and cooks have to clear their dishes, but she's nice enough to help so she can get out sooner. Once everyone is clear she'll lock up the money she collected in a safe and lock the doors behind her as she turns off the radio, lights, and turns on the alarm.

Some people have time to go home and change, while others change right here in the restrooms. Others keep their solid work blacks on. Meredith doesn't mind smelling like Chandler's, like she's been in front of a grill all day, her clothes dense with grease stains and the occasional ungrateful customers' spit. In a few moments, she'll forget about the uniform and only notice what's in front of her. It's normal for her to default to caterer and bartender at parties and bars. She knows them all and she keeps them. She is the one thing she wished and prayed for 10 years ago when she was surviving off the gratitude of her customers.

At Jordan's house she arrives a little later than the rest. Some of her "kids" are already drunk. There's Vicente, a back-of-house young kid who likes to distribute the goods to her front of house. An ugly greasy boy that everyone looks past because he understands the needs of others so well. He'd be a good businessman if he looked better. Maybe he'll mature into a fine young man and find a real business to sell for. The girls arrive dressed down in their skimpy little outfits. Mother Meredith doesn't approve but she doesn't say anything. Some of them stay for a quick drink and a quick high before they leave for a better party or club. The boys come dressed in their skinny jeans and nice shoes.

"Kids and their shoes," she'll say under her breath as she grabs a beer from a fridge outside. It amazes her that these boys have more shoes than she could ever or will ever own.

Now come the minors. The young bussers, hostesses, and the fresh-faced wait staff. This is why she prefers going to bars over coming to these outings. Yet, she still came for a very specific reason. She should've known Jordan would have them over. He enjoys their attention, as they make him seem smarter, more grown, and larger than he really is. It's a fallacy as he uses their naivety for his benefit. He's reliving his high school life through these kids and through this job and always reuses the same jokes and same stories with each new group of kids.

There go the girls. Not 15 minutes into her arriving and some of her children are beginning to leave. The young kids are here and will continue to stay because they have no other source of trouble anywhere else. The older servers begin hitting on the younger girls and each one of them absolutely love the attention they get. They always try to pull their little boy lines on Meredith even though they know better.

It's never hard to leave when you want but it just takes willpower and a strong soul to get up and leave. Just like their jobs. It's hard to let go of the quick cash paying job.

If anyone is short on money, they pick up shifts and make it up in a night. If they have too much money, they can afford to pay people to get off. Even when they get tired of it all, they'll still be seen next door, or at a different bar.

Meredith doesn't say bye to any of her "kids" and just sneaks out. Nobody notices; they are too wrapped up in their own stories to come see her out and Meredith doesn't blame them.

Now she is free to make her way to the Graveyard, the place where she feels most at home, much more her style walking in and seeing everything in its usual form.

Fortunately for her, an old friend is working at the bar. She can ignore everyone else and focus on Sharon. Dependable Sharon, the same Sharon that remembers her drink order from start to finish. A gin and tonic and two amber beers to finish it off. She wishes she could get her attention so that she can vent to her but a Saturday night is rush time for a bar. The nature of the business just to keep the lights on or the water running. Weird fucking hours. Next to her sits a young fellow who just started at Chandler's and is one of Meredith's. He looks over to her slowly with his tired eyes and all Meredith can do is hope that he doesn't come near her or says anything but he does. The conversation she is going to

Anzaldua

have with him is one she's had a hundred times before
this with other workers.

"Hey, how's it going?"

She doesn't respond and just tips the glass and nods
her head.

"How's it working there? How long have you been
here... I mean at Chandler's?"

She thinks to herself *I've been working there too
long.* She tells him she was a manager when she started
but that's a lie and just builds a lie on top of another lie.
She keeps going on about it. Out of rhythm he asks if
she's heard of a recent news story about a young girl who
killed herself. The one in every news cycle.

"Yeah, I heard." She unenthusiastically sips her drink
as she responds.

"Man I think it's crazy how it all went down. People
can get crazy sometimes. I think it's sad how it's all over
the news and online."

This conversation is bringing her down and she nods
at Sharon for one more for the road. She chugs it down
as fast as she can to avoid any more downer talk. After a
hard day, she wants to escape the world, not discuss the
intricacies that leave her vulnerable to actual emotion.
She leaves the cash on the bar with more than enough
for a decent tip, waives at Sharon, and doesn't finish the
conversation as she heads out. She says she'll see the

young man at work tomorrow but probably won't remember they even talked. *Her new kid.*

She walks out just as the drinks are beginning to metabolize inside her. Feeling that buzz, she has to hurry fast before she can no longer safely drive herself home. Though, in reality, she couldn't drive at all beginning three hours ago, still at work.

Finally, after an unreasonable amount of time, she reaches her car. Drunk. Shit faced. She tells herself that she's become quite the professional at driving away safely in this condition. The key is to be extra careful and live two minutes away from everything. She can make it successfully with no scratches on her car, her criminal record, or on anyone else.

Her nightly ritual is to come home, watch TV, and listen to music. She hardly sees her fiancé anymore, the one that supposedly lives with her. When she does see him, they just sit and talk as long as they can. She can't sleep without the sound of his voice, or the feeling of his body sinking the bed lower. When she's alone she can't relax so easily and typically depends on some type of depressant to get her to fall asleep. Sometimes she'll shower but sometimes she won't. Now, she's too drunk to move so she'll just rest on the bed over the covers with a fan on.

"Nothing good happened," she begins to herself, "I don't want to think about it. I'm sure the "kids" will be sharing their great stories for the afternoon. Those stories will be their excuses why they're all late."

She keeps softly speaking to herself as if the sound of her own voice is putting her to sleep. She's pissed knowing she'll have to be at work in a very short and restless four hours. It's not enough time for sleep. She's already gone, and now she's already awake.

Morning in a blink. She can't believe it's been that long. It's cold outside and the TV is still on from when she came home from the bar. Meredith can hear kids leaving their apartment and parents yelling at them to hurry up or they'll be late for church. She remembers how she had friends that went to church but her parents never bothered taking her and because of this, she is indifferent on the subject of faith. She's still in bed on top of a mattress without a frame. She's freezing. Her heart is erupting through her ribs and she can feel the blood flowing like rapids inside her veins and arteries as it makes the headache palpable. It's never a good idea to go to sleep drunk and without layers; as she wants to get up and warm herself but is paralyzed in a drunken stupor. "Did I drink that much?" she wonders. She questions her ability to handle liquor and wonders if she is even the same woman that she was when she left the restaurant. Or the week before. She chokes, she can't breathe anymore, and her shaking becomes violent. She remembers instantly why she stays at her job and why she always wanted to aspire to be something more than her job. It's too early to have such thoughts. All of this goes through her head despite her being awake for only a few seconds. She can't dream anymore when she can barely calm herself. The universe doesn't waste time, so why should she?

She still can't find the will to leave her head and is now already late for her shift. Her breathing worsens. Thoughts flash in her mind.

We are all slaves. We are fighting for survival. Everyone. Our dignity was left at our parents' homes in our childhood fantasies. It's gone.

She can see everything here, ahead, her entire day, and now it's more painful to bear witness. She's not going anywhere. Now her head begins to pound even harder. This headache isn't a normal hangover headache, it's something more. By the time she's able to recognize the sign she's supposed to find, she realizes it's too late. She's already leaving for work again.

IV. The Graveyard

The night lasts an eternity. Daniel, fully soaked in the odors of the fed and the poor kitchen slaves, creeps into the Graveyard. Daniel imagines that he and his fellow workers were cursed from the moment they placed one inch of their being into the restaurant today. He thinks to himself how today got so bad; was it the management, the luck of the draw, or the fact that everyone kept calling in sick? Could be all of the above.

It seemed like today nobody had any empathy for working class as those guests who got the best of each server carried it away. When the restaurant is short on servers, it's overly stressful for those who have the courage to show up. Everything takes longer, including the simple tasks like bussing and seating the tables. It causes a long wait, which can further piss off the famished patrons of the day.

Daniel thinks it's okay to be treated like shit. He thinks the money justifies the poor actions of his guests. This service industry is a world where people come to please others and laugh in vanity while servers like Mary, a soon to be mother and coworker at Chandler's, pick up an extra shift to provide for her unborn child. The extra tips make putting up with complaints, yells, and scowls bearable. Daniel is okay with getting bitched at if it means making 22 dollars an hour.

Out in the Graveyard, Daniel, a young man in his early 20s, waits patiently alone in the bar, drinking and thinking trivial thoughts. Who should he be working for, why should he be working, how does the brain control the finger to grasp the glass and put it near his mouth, and why does alcohol have this calming, soothing effect over him? As he thinks this and wonders how much alcohol is actually in his drinks, he sees his manager, alone in the corner, ordering a drink from Sharon the bartender. She is sitting underneath a bright custom-made neon sign with a cartoon zombie that looks like it was animated by Matt Groening. "Escape the living, party in hell," with "hell" flashing bright red every other second.

Daniel stares at her with an almost empty beer in his hands, trying to understand the aching sharp pain inside his stomach. His chest is hollow with nothing but a small candle inside burning and yearning for something that he doesn't understand. There was never a woman in his life, at least not one to make him stop drinking his beer. He gets the courage to do something he doesn't ever do.

"Hey, how's it goin'?"

She doesn't answer. Daniel doesn't understand why, and his face begins to heat up. His shame is becoming

apparent as he tries to converse with his superior in
hopes of something happening. He wonders how his
new place of employment will affect his life.

"How's it working there? ... How um... how long have
you been here?"

She barely responds loud enough.

"It's okay. I was hired on as a manager. I've been
there too long."

The silence becomes more uncomfortable. He feels
more distant in his thoughts than what he really is.
Awkwardly he brings up a very hot topic.

"Did you hear about that poor girl from a couple of
nights ago?"

"I heard."

"Man, I think it's crazy how it all went down. People
can get crazy sometimes. I think it's sad how it's all over
the news and online, and social media. I can't imagine
what she must've gone through to want to end it all.
Imagine the cops that came on the scene and what they
were thinking. What her parents thought. Her poor
parents. She was so young..."

The alcohol begins to take its toll. Here he is, ranting
and raving about something he cares about, and
Meredith doesn't give a shit. She nods and walks off
while Daniel is left here alone again brooding over the
bar. Daniel wonders why anyone would ever look at her

like a motherly figure, or a big sister. Maybe because she looks like shit all the time. Frantic with frizzled hair and bags under her eyes just like a new mother caring for a newborn at all hours of the night. He's not her baby.

The girl that killed herself affected him on a personal level. He fights depression everyday and understands the meaning of a bad day, the meaning of being alone in a room full of smiles. Being a server helps this young man understand the idea that people who come in his life can leave just as quickly. Little moments, minute memories that are easily forgotten with drinks. Moments in his mind can last as long as he lets them; in his mind he can live through the most tragic deaths over and over while others have the gift to forget.

The industry provides a vessel for those with issues to expel their demons and wait for another night to pass by. He surveys all of this eating and drinking. Prideful celebrating is useless when society itself has nothing worth celebrating. Every day in this city there is somebody who is killed and nobody tips more than 13% on their bill. This is a city built on money; the power of salvation seems so insignificant, like their fake million dollar tips they leave.

Ironically, the Christian doctrine to give to the needy does not override their personal endeavors. Of course, this is assuming Christians are more inclined to help others before they can take care of their own needs. John the Baptist preached in Luke that "Whoever has two tunics should share with him who has none, and whoever has food should do the same." Daniel takes it a step further: he shares his fucking tunics. The people he waits on don't share shit. The people around him don't share anything at all. He begins to fixate around this thought.

Daniel is on the verge of an anxiety attack. This is what he thinks every day as he was brought up to be religious, but because of the severity of his disorder, Jesus is about to leave his heart. His heart begins to gallop through his body, and his drink is getting lower. He orders a quick shot to try to defuse the bomb, but something else carries his mind away.

A young woman struts through the door with a uniform that isn't supposed to show off anything that she's willing to exploit herself. Standing in black tights, not much taller than the bar tables, she wears a grass green top that asks for the certain kind of attention she wants. It's not too revealing, and shows no cleavage but it enhances her curves and shows her to be slightly smaller than what she really is as it bells out on the bottom.

Seeing her calms Daniel. He takes one look in those emeralds of eyes and forgets all that he was thinking. Those eyes shine at him, even in such a dark place. He feels serene and has recollected himself just moments before he freaks out. He remembers that he went to high school with her. It seems too cliché to use this as a conversation starter but he *does* remember her at school. The way she looked and the way her face was slightly smaller back then. The thickness on her face is perfectly placed to enhance her smile as she walks over to him. With a pure and simple light-hearted face she glides across the dive bar right next to him.

"I remember you!" he yells over the chatter and the Depeche Mode album playing in the background. She is bashful and smiles from ear to ear. She licks her lips.

"I remember you too! What's new?" she asks as if she cares.

"Work, school, drinks. Nothing really."

"Are you still wanting to do your music?"

"Music? Wow, I...you remember that?" He didn't realize he was so memorable. Music was something he thought about a lot. He hums unimagined beats, rhythms, and lyrics in his head as he's fixing salads and drinking alone in a bar. The fact that she remembered something that he forgot defeats him almost immediately.

"Of course I do. It's all I ever heard from you," she responds.

"Yeah. Well, no. Not anymore. It's not a real career choice according to my mom and dad."

"Be a music teacher! Lots of people teach music. Especially to rich kids. Rich parents want music and enrichment for their children!"

"No, they don't. I guess I could've done that." He smirks, and chuckles awkwardly looking around and sipping on his drink waiting for her next line.

"Why not?"

"Yeah. Well I guess I'll change my major tomorrow. My mind and major."

"From what? What are ya studying now?"

"Business finance management."

"That sounds like shit."

He smiles from ear to ear watching her sway to the rhythm of "Master and Servant."

"It is!"

He can't believe it; how shitty his decision sounds to him now that he's said it out loud. It was always in his head that going to school was enough. Getting a higher education. It didn't matter that he was studying something boring to him because he's trying to stop himself from sulking away. Depression works funny like this: misery loves company. Never is this statement truer than when two depraved souls join in union. It's sadly beautiful when people get along with one another because of their circumstances.

Mary and Daniel have both travelled the road not travelled and can speak of the scary monsters they grew up with. They can feed off each other and their eyes tell the tales of their darkest nightmares. Mary orders what Daniel is having and while they wait for the drink they continue the bullshit small talk that is only reserved for their customers.

"You come here a lot?" Daniel asks.

"No."

"What are you doing here?"

"I was going to meet up with a friend. I just got off. He's taking *forever*."

Upon hearing the word "he" Daniel's heart drops. His palms become soap-slippery and wet as he wipes them on his dirty pants.

"Who is *he*?"

"A good friend of mine. He's having boyfriend issues and wanted to meet up. I'm not sure he's going to meet after all. His boyfriend is really jealous, so he might've flaked. You know how people in relationships are, like, really hung up on each other. Well, people in good relationships anyway."

Daniel's weight is lifted as he exhales his relief. Mary's drink is put in front of her. She drinks almost half of it within five seconds. He's glad that "he" isn't some boyfriend of hers, or a date, or a fuck buddy. This now presents him with a wonderful opportunity.

"I don't really drink much," she continues "but he needed an ear, and another woman's perspective."

"Is he the woman?"

They both laugh sensing the dry humor. Mary's eyes follow the sound back to the jukebox wondering if Daniel has the balls to offer her something more than the Graveyard.

"He can be a woman sometimes. Not saying that all gay guys are like that. Just some. But drag queens are awesome."

"I wouldn't know." Daniel says as if he's losing interest. Mary, sensing this, decides to be bold.

"You should go to a show. I'll take you."

"Why would we go to a drag show?"

"I've got a lot of boyfriends that would be excited to meet you." Mary chuckles. "Not really. One of my favorite cousins is gay. It was hard for him coming out to his family, but love wins in my eyes...Wow. *That* was corny. I'm just saying that I was there for him when no one else was. No. Drag shows are fun. We would have fun. I'll take you."

Mary inches closer to him. Their drinks touch. The condensation of the two half-drunk beers meet on the table. Daniel takes a huge gulp, almost finishing his beer.

"That's not corny, that's pretty awesome."

They continue to keep their conversations light as they both hide their dark and similar thoughts from each other. They are both disturbed souls but neither knows about it or how deep their thoughts are capable of going. How the hell do you tell someone you're manically depressed and clinically insane? Their conversation slowly becomes more authentic, accelerating to blunt opinions. When they were younger, both Daniel and Mary never would have dreamed to approach one another. Tonight, their faces brought a familiarity and nostalgia to each other, as if a friendly face in the crowd were saying "hey, I, too, remember when times were a bit simpler." Their high school days didn't seem so complex after all. Their youth seems like nothing in comparison to what the real world can do.

Daniel's heart beats faster and faster. Blood rushes to his face again. This time, it's different. It's a euphoric feeling. Mary feels the same way. She is putting herself out for him. She feels like she wants to go home with him. She doesn't do this because she's slutty, or a whore, but out of the thought that the only way to be close with someone is simply to take that chance. They continue to talk and annoy the bartender because they don't order any more drinks but instead waste time on a Saturday night in her bar. It gets later and the bar empties out.

Soon, the chatter softens, and the background synthpop is the only sound as it echoes in the emptiness with the slurred chatter. Everything at the Graveyard appears less dark than before. Happier. Drunker.

"What do you have going on after this? You should come back to my house," Daniel suggests.

"What?"

"I mean to talk. If you're not too tired, I know it's late, but... I enjoyed talking with you tonight." He pauses and looks at her, examining her expression. "I don't want it to stop."

"Do you still live in your mansion?" She smiles.

"I do."

She raises her glass to her mouth contemplating his offer. She takes a drink that lasts for years only to see if Daniel is going to back out on his word

"That'd be nice. My friend never came by. Maybe I'll check on him on my way."

They continue to converse and make small talk, both not yet revealing anything with substance. Mary takes a seat and orders one more round before they close out their tab. Daniel's leg accidentally grazes Mary's. Awkwardly, they apologize and look down. Mary is flushed with this last drink just enough to do her in. She pushes the drink aside and asks Daniel to finish it off. He feels like lingering around here is rude.

Presumptuous. He moves the drink closer to him. He sips it where she first did. They lock eyes with one another and truly feel something new; an anxiety attack without the anxiety.

Mary whispers, "Let's go now. I don't want to be alone. It'd be nice to be with somebody...who cares."

Daniel tries to hide his buzz. He leans into her. He almost loses his balance but is able to gain his composure once he realizes the buzz is coming from Mary and not the alcohol, although it could be a contributing power to his newly found confidence.

"I care."

With those simple words, Mary shows her teeth as her eyes get smaller.

"Let's go."

Daniel's house is as massive as Mary remembers. None of his past depression matters as he takes her to his humble home. Daniel thinks of Mary as flawless, and still in the back of his mind he knows what his mother and father would say if they found a girl in their house. A girl like her.

Once they get inside, they each lower their guards, unzipping their insecurities. They take apart one another, piece by piece, word by word. Their words penetrate the other, they become one in the moment's conversation.

Mary looks outside onto the city's busy streets. A train blows its horn nearby several times almost like it's trying to wake up the sleeping people in a quiet neighborhood. Daniel's house sits high on top of a hill on the corner of a new development still waiting to be complete. Mary stares out the window. Her arms wrap around herself feeling uneasy about the occurrences of the week.

"Can you imagine killing yourself?" she asks. "Like, what is so troubling that it can't be fixed? What is so dark inside that nothing can save you but death?"

"I try not to think about it."

"But you do, right?" She looks at him in his eyes. Eyes that she has seen in the mirror when she wakes up. Filled with tension. Filled with questions and unanswered explanations that erode her insides.

"I mean," Daniel grabs her arm. "I don't ever *think* about doing it to myself. Maybe hypothetically, but nothing serious. I think about it though. Like what would happen."

"Do you think it's selfish?" Mary's eyes gloss over almost like she wants to cry but can't form enough tears to stream down her face. The thought of death scares her. She hasn't lived a life she is particularly proud of, feeling like she's accomplished nothing.

"I think it's a failed cry for help. I think that maybe they aren't *really* thinking about doing it. You hear stories of people that survive it and they are glad they didn't go through with it after all."

"Can you say that about this girl? Getting abused. Teased. It's just so sad."

"Maybe she regretted what she did. The only way out to her was death. She was scared. She didn't want to face what was ahead."

"Yeah. But I've heard stories about people killing other people and then turning themselves in. Like a guy who killed his wife. He knew he was troubled. He knew he was twisted. He turned himself in because he knew he was going to be a danger to himself and other people. "

"Sure. They get sympathy and *then* they get help. For killing someone?"

"Sympathy? Maybe if they looked like they were sorry. Or even said that."

"Not a lot of that going around, I don't think."

The two begin to talk about their deep philosophies on life and change subjects often, going from the girl's death to understanding the psychology of killing to where and how they grew up. Even if they don't truly know what they are talking about, they know that they are speaking their mind. Mary is upset about the daily news she keeps seeing. About the constant fear of negative change taking place on Earth. About the war, about the violence, the starvation of society, climate change, politics, epidemics, and everything the world on a screen wants you to be scared of. Tonight, she feels shielded from the world around her. Tonight, Daniel is there.

So here they are, giving each other the attention they need and sitting in a hardly used bed inside Daniel's room. This was more than enough for them to look forward to a tomorrow they both used to dread. Together, they compliment each other. They left the Graveyard to be together in a different world. A world where they can be alone, where they can fully understand their absolute truth. Daniel and Mary exist and, in a world of chaos, only *they* matter.

The beauty that is completely hidden in the dark is completely visible when a ray of sunshine leaks. After a full night of conversation, it seems as if the sun itself is signaling to them that all of their troubles had brought them here to meet. So respectfully that the first ray of light would cross those beautiful hill-green eyes that Daniel had ever seen before. Then her chest. Then her legs. Not minding the time, they smile one last time and embrace each other. Even the Devil was once an angel; it's only a matter of understanding. And while all the stars in the known universe display humanity's insignificance, for this moment, they both know their purpose. Tonight, they are very much significant. Tonight, they are together.

Last Call

My glass is empty; it just sits there.
It doesn't notice what I see so
Why should I care about
The vessels around me lusting about
Doing their share
For attention.

Just living free; and all I do
Is stare at the girl with
The small skirt who dances
For hours wanting free drinks,
Not knowing the hurt
That will happen later.

She will only know the devil
that took her away from the life
she thought she knew: the being
where she came from—I wait to get another
Sip of hope, and the bars wait for tips
where our dignity is taken.

V. Rolling: Molly

The shift is over but the parties are not. Three girls left Jordan's place because nothing there was worth staying for. Not the little boys, not the weak drinks, not the silly perverted jokes; these ladies were living for a real party far away from the realities of a sheltered world. They would find it by searching their phones to find out where each other's "real" friends were at. They walk to Stephanie's car with a false sense of purpose, each turning on cameras from their smartphones to check on makeup. They all pose for various pictures and selfies before they actually get in the car and turn on the ignition. After several attempts to get the "look" they want, the girls post them around various forms of social media. Despite the temperature dropping by the minute, they wear clothes that show their curves and skin under their long coats. All of them know they are going to get hot tonight. Off they go, into the dark street, lit by warm lamps that give off an illusion of a real heat source. The strobing of the lamps light up the car like a dance floor as the girls laugh about their day, making fun of customers' ridiculous requests while adding a slice of their own dark humor.

They're living for themselves and nothing else. Earlier, when they all arrived at their double shift in the morning, they were already looking forward to the nightlife that nobody else in the restaurant knew about. Gez, a young lady, but the oldest of the bunch at 24, wears a tight red V-neck dress so short you can't be sure she's wearing anything under her long coat. Natalie, the youngest at 19, wears a two-piece neon green outfit that closely resembles a swimsuit, with neon boy shorts. An outfit she found at the local lingerie and sex shop. Something that a go-go dancer would wear at a cheap bar or underground dance club. Barely 21-year-old Stephanie is in red and green sequined bottoms with a solid black tank top that enhances her cleavage and exposes her midriff. She convinces Gez to drive because she knows where they are going and she can get them there faster. That, and she doesn't want to be held responsible for any accidents that may or may not occur. They ride and listen to deep house and dubstep. The filthy bass, strong kick on the downbeats, and the complex chords relax these girls into a playful ease. The essence of dance music makes them move intensely and provokes them to take further action on their natural high. Add a bit of Jolly Molly, as they call it, and they are taken to a high from which they don't want to come down.

"Wanna get jolly?" Stephanie suggests.

"Imma get *jolly!*" yells Natalie. Gez rolls her eyes. She can't believe they just said that: *jolly. How fucking stupid,* she thinks, but once she gets over herself she remembers it was her that thought up the expression and joins them in their absurdities.

They continue to drive and prepare themselves for a wonderful "jolly" experience. Everyone except Gez takes a pill. She's driving now and doesn't want to be affected yet. The night will be long, and she's experienced enough to know when and how to take it.

Stephanie doesn't get high often; she's actually a rookie when it comes to party drugs. Only sticks to pot, and has yet to discover the more highly concentrated dab. Doing that would leave her paralyzed if, of course, it is the right amount of concentration. Gez introduced her to other fun recreational items: the sedatives, the stimulants, the psychadelics, the uppers, the downers, and the shit that turns you straight up into a fucking blade of grass. Gez was always enticing her on a subliminal level with her lingering care free scent of smoke, weed, and alcohol. Gez recalls a long, exhausting day at work, while she observed Stephanie crying on a table while rolling silverware. She asked if she had ever experienced the relief of total freedom from all the pain she's suffered.

At first Stephanie didn't believe her, nor did she care to ask what she meant. She seemed intrigued by her proposal.

"Don't feel bad about today. You know what it's like not to care? I bet I could make you forget about it all."

It technically isn't seduction if someone already wants it.

"Look. Take some of this, on me." She handed Stephanie a white pill. "You'll feel better in an hour or so. " She winked at her and strolled off into the kitchen. Stephanie didn't understand what she meant by that until two hours later.

Before it hit she was fighting back and knee pain all day long on a double shift. Her dinner shift was much more brutal than lunch. Once she got home at her parents' three-bedroom house, she decided to take her pill. She didn't know what or how to anticipate what was going to happen next. She was calm and did her nightly routine.

Once she was in the shower, it hit her.

The water slowed down. It suddenly became calm. She felt like a speedster. Like The Flash, moving faster than sound, she was able to perceive time for what it really was: nothing. Water was dripping on her naked body and she could feel every single droplet and could identify every spot where it landed. Her hands felt slippery like silk. Soap never moisturized so much. After her shower she dried herself with a towel for ten minutes as she wanted to fill every thread on that piece of drying cloth. The towel was a chinchilla and it was even talking to her about how cool Gez was. She walked out of the bathroom and saw a brand new house lit with vibrant crimson all around her. She got herself an ice water and crunched every ice cube slowly, feeling the intense and refreshing blizzard it created inside her body. She slithered out of the towel and lay naked in bed, something she never did because her parents slept next door. Every fiber gave her a deep impulse that synced with her heart. She couldn't stop tossing in her bed and chewing ice until she came down and fell asleep.

She dreamed of meeting Morgan Freeman in a haunted house and found it offensive. When she woke up the next day she was freezing. She was embarrassed because her father came in on her passed out, with her left breast exposed. Once awake, she couldn't get herself to go to work or to carry out the plans she made the previous day. A bit confused and down, she blamed that on the bad night she had at work that still lingered in her mind.

Stephanie heard how it feels to be dancing while jolly, so she decided to come tonight to experience the love herself.

Gez rolls on a weekly basis. She's been doing it since she was 16 years old. She took a trip to London and had the best first experience. She could never find anything quite like what they sold overseas. Now she is in a constant search for the best trips and is still searching to find a high that's just right.

Natalie is a poser. She's never tried it before, but she's trying to fit in for the first time of her life. She'll say and do anything for attention. During her first week at Chandler's nobody knew who she was. Nobody remembered her because she had no distinguishable features. She didn't wear make-up, she had brown eyes and black hair with fair skin. She was so forgettable that once she began to model her appearance after Gez, she looked like a different person. Everyone thought the bland girl quit and was replaced by a new punk girl named Natty.

Once they reach the house party in some run down neighborhood, they're slightly buzzed from Jordan's, but Molly hasn't kicked in yet. The three girls freeze as they walk into the house. The house is located in the central area of the city surrounded by train tracks, bridges, and welding factories. People are dancing inside the house, as made apparent by their silhouettes through the window. Natalie and Gez walk and talk together as Stephanie double checks to make sure all of her car doors are locked and her valuables are secure.

"This area is kinda sketch!" Stephanie whispers to Gez as she drinks a 40 oz of Bud Ice she conveniently pulled out of her oversized Lacoste bag.

"It's okay...I grew up down the street. I know everyone in this part of town. No need to worry."

Natalie is new to the scene and has never seen anything like this. The rundown house. The people dressed the way they were. The lack of hygiene. She walks in and immediately clutches her jacket, sticking out like a white lady in a black church. She is by far the prettiest, youngest, and most innocent there. She notices in the corner a rat running under the couch and into the wall. She is disgusted and uneasy about the experience. "Whose house is this?" she asks.

"It's my cousin's." Gez takes a drink of her own 40 oz and downs what's left of it. She carefully places the oversized bottle in a cinder block that sits right next the porch. "He's cool. He lives here alone, so we're gonna just crash here tonight. He'll take care of us. You're off tomorrow, right?"

"Yeah." Stephanie is wondering if coming along was a good idea after all. Maybe she would've been better off working in the morning, earning money to move out instead of coming to this nasty-ass house.

"Aaron picked up my shift. He needed the extra cash so I let him."

"You'll need the time to recover!" Gez laughed mischievously.

Stephanie follows them inside, beeping her lock button three times in a row as if it makes the car more secure. As *if.* The girls prance and skip inside the entryway, which isn't much of an entryway. Once inside there is a small living room packed with sweaty bodies and a stench. Walk 10 paces forward to the kitchen and dining room. Beyond that is the restroom. There are three bedrooms, all on the right side. Each the same size, completely joined together. There are more people than the house can hold—all of them dressed up in bright and revealing colors and outfits. All of the windows are open to let the cool air come in, but the heat from the bodies is enough to keep it steamy. Gez looks around and gives the other two girls a quick tour of the house. It seems unnecessary, seeing as the entire house is barely 970 sq ft. Gez creeps to the restroom in the back of the house. Once she locks the door, she takes out a pill and dissolves it in a small cup she got from the kitchen table. She then takes out a syringe from her bag. She slurps the liquid up into the syringe and pulls up her dress and pulls down her thong. She sticks the syringe inside her anus so that she can feel it faster and stronger. She isn't going to wait for it and she doesn't have to. She has trouble pulling her dress back down and when she walks out her ass is hanging out, but she enjoys the breeze.

It takes the other two girls 15 solid minutes for them to feel the effect. Before that they were talking to each other, wondering why they were here in this ugly, cold, and smelly house. Nobody is cute and they wish that they would've stayed at Jordan's house. At least there, it was in a safer part of the town. They notice water stains on the ceiling and wooden panels that are tearing off. What the fuck *is* this place? The foundation on the floor is cracked and they can feel under the linoleum. Someone is sharing blow, and Natalie sees someone in the corner of the entry stab their own foot with a needle and just pass out. There is a stench of body odor and Stephanie is pretty sure she just saw a cat cough up a hairball in the kitchen. Nobody knows who the cat belongs to or where it came from. None of what the people are doing makes any sense to them. They're just moving with no rhythm and dancing to loud, hard, awful, music, not minding any of the imperfections of the house. It is filthy and they are getting anxious to leave. They try to get Gez's attention, but she is too busy dancing in one of the three rooms. Natalie is trying to walk outside to smoke a cigarette in anger but Stephanie tries to stop her from storming out.

She grabs her by the arm, and an irritable Natalie turns to her. As she touches her she realizes something.

"Your skin is so. *Sooo.* Very. Slimy."

"I know." Natalie feels it. For the first real time.

"You look amazing. Have you always been so beautiful?" She continues to stroke her arm and gazes deep into her very normal looking eyes.

"I... don't remember," she starts to crack up. Uncontrollably.

The once loathsome house turns into the greatest night club in a blink of an eye. Several girls are walking around in their cute cheeky little underwear. Some of them are in boyshorts, and the slightly chubby are in hiphuggers. Everyone looks amazing. Some of the guys, though few and far between, have opted to remove their shirts since the girls arrived. Their chiseled jaws, muscular arms, and ripped bodies make the girls feel like they are on the set of the movie *300*. The girls are ready to be manhandled. The men obviously took care to ensure each pompadour was perfect; the long hair tousled, and the short hair barely spiked to perfection. Of course their obviously malnourished bodies look glistening to them.

"I bet they manscape," Stephanie says to Natalie. Gez's cousin comes up to them. He moves his hands in the pocket of his brown shorts to adjust himself

accordingly. To them, he looks like a god with all 5'11"
towering over.

"Hey, you're my cousin's friends, right? Glad you
could make it. I'm feeling good. Are you feeling good?
I've been doin' this since Thursday. Gez! It's about time
you join me!"

There is a boy sitting down—he is just feeling himself
on the loveseat. He is wearing a shirt with Hello Kitty's
face with a bullet hole through her head. Stephanie finds
it so hilarious she can't stop laughing. She joins him on
the love seat, trying to think of her opening line.
Something to start any kind of conversation.

"Did I work with you?" asks Stephanie.

"I don't think so."

"I remember you. We worked at Dirty Murphy's.
Next to Chandler's. I wanted to ask you out to the roller
rink or some shit."

"I don't think I did. Wait... what's your name?"

The boy starts laughing and leans in to kiss her. It
doesn't take long for Stephanie to get what she secretly
wants. At first Stephanie resists, but after a split second
she wants to experience a different kiss, one that, when
high, feels completely new. Their mouths are dry and his
hands are rough, but to her it is entirely different than
anything she has ever felt. His tongue flaps around
quickly, at the same time massaging her teeth. His hands

trickle down her sequins, a sensation they both equally enjoy. It was a new first time.

Gez is feeling good, laughing to herself as she watches this random guy fumble with the texture of Stephanie's sequin bottoms. She feels so good that all her tension and frustration of her awful day seem to melt away. Melt. *Away.* Everything is fucking great. She is listening to the *best* music in the world in the *greatest* house with the *best* people. They look as if they beat cancer, discovered world peace, and found the meaning of life. She pops another pill. She knows that will be enough to last her into the morning and to keep going. She screams out loud and throws her hands up. The minor chords and deep kicks keep Natalie entertained. She analyzes the structure of how a good piece of music is spliced together. She taps her foot to the 4/4 time signature. The crescendos and the chord progression right before the drop. The 130 beats per minute. She starts to slowly exercise her freedom to dance.

Stephanie was still making out when Gez slapped her.

"I see you. Gettin' caught in the act!"

"Or lettin' the act gettin' caught in you?"

They simultaneously fake laugh at each other. And then they really start laughing. And now they can't stop. Laughing feels so good when you're jolly. Everything feels so good: the cold concrete on bare feet, the brisk

air against the sweat on a steamy body. Complete joy.
Complete harmony: everything is perfect. Nothing is
wrong with the world they live in, not tonight. Nothing is
going to bring them down... at least not for a few more
hours...

The boy on the couch grabs Stephanie to dance in
the middle of the living room. On the speakers plays a
funky guitar riff with strong bass and synths overlaying.

wikawakawikawaka BOOM BOOM.

The music replicates a cross between blues, disco,
and modern dance.

Wikawaka BEEP BEEP wikawaka BEEP BEEP.

She turns her back towards him and begins grinding
on him slowly, seductively, and purposefully.

BOOM kick hithat BOOM kick hithat BOOM kick hithat BOOM kick
hithat beep beep Drop.

As her ass rubs against the front of his jeans, his body
can't help but respond to the friction. She moves her
body to control his direction. She plays with him, teases
him, and once the song is over they walk off into the
night, not to be seen for at least 14 minutes.

Happiness is streaming on Gez's face and she's
talking about nothing. She tells the story about her first
time experimenting in London, one that her cousin has
heard so many times. She tells it to a young couple, a
drunk girl, and Natalie. They are all amused by her

recited humor and one liners. She gets a little coarse towards the end but nobody seems to mind.

The sun comes up as they are coming down. The smell returns, but worse than before. The people have deep shadows under their eyes and everyone looks and feels like a zombie. Gez is still rolling but Stephanie and Natalie are down and almost out. Natalie is confused. The air is a lot more suffocating than it was in the dark. Stephanie is scared out of her own mind. She is sore all over—her chest, her ass, her thighs. But the pain there is sharp and raw. Nothing she'd experienced before. Her fingers run inconspicuously under her skirt emerging with a thick, slimy substance. Natalie is freezing and they both approach Gez and tell her they are going to leave. The bliss both girls were feeling moments ago is gone. They are both dead in the eyes and just want rest. In the somber car ride home the bright sun blinds them both with the obvious truth that their choices will lead to peril. With no appreciation for the warmth, they crawl back home in Stephanie's old '99 Honda. Natalie is dropped off at the front of her apartment complex, unconventionally sad that Stephanie is leaving. They'll see each other soon but it doesn't matter at this moment in time. Once Stephanie comes home her mind is hazy and her heart is heavy with remorse. She feels like her whole life is a mistake. Her whole reason for existence is completely unclear and for once in her life she is scared of taking the next step. She is sleep deprived and sober: the thought of getting caught high by her parents is unreasonably scary. The thought of anything is scary. The world isn't beautiful and everyone is full of hate. She is crashing hard and has a different outlook on the world. The thought of facing anything real isn't worth the time. When she comes home she puts on pants over her shorts for warmth and lies on her sofa. The TV is still showing the news from when her parents left for brunch. On it she sees propaganda about violence, crimes, poverty, war, and a declining economy. She doesn't have the energy to change the channel but watches and listens. She sees the clip from a local story about a girl who killed herself because of some bullying shit. She worked at a restaurant to help pay for her parents' debts. It's so hard to accept the world for what it is, and Stephanie, like that young girl, doesn't want to accept the truth. The truth that her world is not going to change until it's too late.

Stephanie decides that she doesn't want to feel like this. Fortunately for her, the effects are only temporary and she will feel better in a few days and back to her normal optimistic self. But first, it's off to get ready for work because her shift begins in two hours.

The same cannot be said for Gez. Her mind is so delusional that it creates a better world for her to live in. When she comes down, she'll find something to help her feel better about herself. Another substance, or maybe more of the same substance. She hasn't quite decided yet. She'll continue to complain and she'll continue to use until she wakes from the catatonic states she has permanently put herself in. It is surprisingly hard to forgive herself for the small things she will or won't do in life, but when she does, she'll find that moving on is easier than it seems in her head. That is, if she can get out of her head, but she doesn't and when she wakes up she continues to roll. She'll continue until she's forced to stop partying.

Suddenly it's early Monday morning. The sun has yet to paint the sky and the children are walking to their bus stops while Gez is still rolling. She's been doing it all weekend. Her hair is greasy, and her body reeks of hunger and alcohol. With a combination of other things, to her it's a feeling of invincibility. She's sitting there outside of her cousin's house, laughing at this kid who tripped over a crack in the cement but didn't fall over. The air smells of rain and it's much warmer than it was this weekend. At the start she had complete control over everything; she was smiling and laughing, and now the loneliness is setting in. The universe of emotions she rejects will come rushing to her any moment now. Until then, she's going to take it all in and enjoy her high while she still can.

VI. Prep

It's 5:29 am. The restaurant is completely dark. Outside four men wait by the door for the manager to open it. He is, of course, running late. Ice covers the grass from the moisture of the cold night but the weatherman says the afternoon will warm it up a bit. The men wait, drinking their coffee out of their canisters and smoking their cigarettes. One of the four men was here last night closing the restaurant. Vicente, the youngest one, even decided to go out to a party after work and only got two hours of sleep. He never changed or showered before he got here. He still has a ketchup stain on his pants from yesterday. It is not certain if he is sober or not.

"I thought Mexicans were always the ones runnin' late?" one of them says as they see Charlie, the opening manager, finally show up in his brand new luxury smart car. He struggles to open the door and get out of his car. He can barely get his seat belt off and, despite the freezing weather, he begins to break out in a sweat as it takes a few tries of pushing his large body out for him to emerge out of the small car. Like a glob of hot peanut butter, slow, and gooey. Rolling and rolling and rolling his body goes. As the four men stare at him, laughing among themselves, they wait patiently, watching the blob move. He's late as usual and also probably still drunk from the night before. Upper management at Chandler's always suggests you show up 10 minutes before you are scheduled, not two minutes, not one minute, not five seconds, but 10 whole minutes. As he stumbles, Juan, Julian, Adolfo, and Vicente are eager to start their day in the best way possible. More can be said about these back of house workers than the kids that run the chain of restaurants. They have work ethic.

The back of house staff is the core of the restaurant. They put the food together. They create the primary element that brings people in: sustenance. The four amigos get along with everyone; there is no drama, there is no complaining, and there is no time for anything else but the duties at hand. They work, do the job they are so lowly paid for, eat, sleep, and do the job over and over again until they are told to go home before they make more money in overtime than the servers.

They are working for the American Dream. That one idea that stole the hearts of immigrants all over the world. You can come from nothing, start from nothing, and come to this country and *be* something. Juan wants to be something.

At 19 years old, Juan is no older than any of the kids that are from the front of house. He is clean, tall, dark, and of course handsome. He looks older than 19 but that's probably because his age is creeping from his soul to his physical appearance. He enjoys the simple pleasures of America such as her justice system, law enforcement, and an endless supply of eye candy. Juan is from Ciudad Juarez, so getting here wasn't hard, as all he needed to do was drive about 630 miles east. He wanted to get away and his family awarded him the opportunity to leave because he showed the most promise of all his siblings. He left moments before the politics of the border became temperamental. Close the borders, build a wall, kick them out. All the wonderful rhetoric that can build fear out of an average American. He was told to stay where he was and wait until things got better, but conditions never improved and have only escalated, especially in recent years and now he is scared to return because he won't be able to come back.

Juan is incredibly intelligent and if given the opportunity, he would excel in mathematics and physics. However, because of his broken English and legal status in the US, and lack of information on how the American system works, Juan is stuck. He works for himself and aspires to go to college, gain his citizenship, and sleep with a beautiful, thick, white Texas girl, and in the United States, he'll continue to have these opportunities.

The manager finally gets to the door and the day can begin.

"Mornin' 'migos."

"Good morning," they all say one by one. The doors open to a dark kitchen that is cold and smells like bleach. The stainless steel is stainless and every single dish is clean and ready for its purpose. The men walk to the time clock and one by one they enter their four digit employee number and clock in.

Time Entry 5:45AM

Time Entry 5:45AM

Time Entry 5:45AM

Time Entry 5:46AM

"Hey *jefe*," says Julian, "You better pay me for that minute. Bout you show up earlier tomorrow guey."

"Yeah, I'll put it on my to-do list." Charlie says with a smile.

Julian is the middleman in getting people over the border. He helps people start a new life in the States. He is a legal citizen who knows how to bring over cheap and effective labor to big restaurant chains that have no interest in background checks. He works for his family, has two sons, and wants both of them to have a life that he didn't; a life with dignity and respect, and without any corruption. He works endless days to help his sons get what they really deserve. He also makes sure that nobody screws with him and his workers. He is the kitchen king, and every employee there knows that if they mess with someone from his staff, his crew, his *familia*, they will be starting trouble. *La Raza—su gente.* If management disrespects him in any way, the entire kitchen will walk out in a moment's notice. He is the voice that communicates, the voice of reason, the ambassador to keep peace, and the bridge between two cultures that have yet to attempt to solve any issues inside and outside of the kitchen.

The day begins swiftly. Charlie and his staff of four work in complete harmony. The machine turns on well before most of the world is even thinking about their first meal. These men put their rest aside to assure that lunch and dinner are created with culinary perfection. The steaks marinate, the stoves hiss on before the fire erupts, and Adolfo washes and cuts the vegetables in perfect portions for the soup..

Adolfo is a culinary artist. He takes pride in his work and treats each ingredient as if it came from his own home kitchen. He was brought here with his wife by a *coyote* that nobody else was desperate enough to trust. The *coyote* failed to keep Adolfo safe but was more focused on his wife instead. He didn't execute his contracted work and instead attempted to ditch Adolfo with Border Control. However, this attempt would bring him to a poetic justice, as he was apprehended instead. In a panic, Adolfo and his wife needed to make a quick choice to either get away in one direction and run, or to just cross and hope for the best. Adolfo was patient and wanted to wait in hiding but his wife was arrogant and ran for the free land in an attempt to find her lover. She was caught. Adolfo wasn't surprised and witnessed her being taken away by ICE. He didn't give a shit and was happier for this. He tells his workers that his wife was a controlling bitch and that she had it coming.

After Charlie gets the team going, he walks into the office to take care of the paperwork. Boring shit really: product orders, food costs, portions, inventory. But these mundane details are things that will lead to another good bonus if they are done correctly. Once he's done with the bureaucratic nonsense he walks to his kitchen and admires the workers in his employ. He pours himself a cup of coffee from the same coffee machine they use to serve their customers and sips on it hot and black. He walks to the walk-in and takes out the salmon. He gets his personal knife set and measures the weight of each piece with pin point accuracy. He slices and moves his knife like a concert violinist, swiftly and aggressively,

making it seem easier than it actually is. For a brief
moment he remembers the dream to be a culinary chef,
cooking eclectic dishes in his restaurant in the heart of a
huge city filled with culture. *Maybe Chicago*, he had
thought. The types of restaurants that invent new ways to
enjoy and love food; the places where they serve foam on
a miniature plant or some beef turned into a bubble.
He's not upset about it; he still loves his job. He wants to
save up some more money to open a food truck and
when he does, he's going to take Adolfo with him.
Dreams don't come easy to entitled people: instead they
come with hard work, passion, desire, and discipline.
Oftentimes, people confuse discipline and inspiration
only because it takes one to make the other; starting
artists don't know that, but Charlie knows this all too
well. In order to make something happen, and gain the
inspiration to move forward, he must be well versed in
his culinary skills. Until then...

While Charlie is preparing various seafoods for the
day, Vicente approaches him from the side. He's slurring
and his eyes are heavy. A line of cocaine would do him
some good right about now, especially because his shift
doesn't end for another nine hours assuming that
everyone shows up. For now, a multi-hour energy drink
will have to do the trick.

The brilliant culinary minds at Chandler's Casual Eatery include alcoholic ingredients for their food. Vicente needs a bottle of bourbon, two bottles of red wine, and some draft beer for the recipes he is going to prepare for the lunch shift. The beer will be used in the beer-battered fried chicken, shrimp, and onion rings. The wine for some of the pasta sauces. Bourbon for the rich and sweet sauce that is ladled over a grilled chicken dish and is also used to marinate some beef for the stew. These ingredients require management and supervision to ensure no thefts take place and to prevent drinking on the job.

Vicente, born in the US but raised by the same people he clocks in with, can't seem to stay out of trouble. He is a greasy man with a face covered in pimples, large pores, and scars. As a young boy Vicente was bullied for this reason. His bully teased him, called him names, made fun of his parents, his facial features, and vandalized heirloom artifacts of his own culture. Over time he became filled with rage and retaliated with his fists and rocks to his tormentor's face. Vicente lashed out and kicked his ass so hard that the young bully needed reconstructive surgery.

After this, Vicente was forever known as the "Mexican kid who beat up the white boy on the football team." Nobody was innocent but the masses seem to enjoy picking sides.

Two wrongs always create more wrongs. Of course after the incident, Vicente was sent to a corrections center and came out more dangerous and vicious. The chip on the shoulder became a gaping hole of frustration. Now, a stubborn veteran of a class and societal war, he purposefully embraced the stereotype and took advantage of the surrounding analyses of his unperceptive coworkers. His war is being fought with the community around him and for survival. With income from the cheap weed he deals to the servers and to the harder narcotics he pushes to them, he gets himself some nicer things and is the richest and most corrupt person that works in the back of house at Chandler's Casual Eatery.

With all the money he makes, he still doesn't take the time to set up a dermatologist appointment. He knows who he is, and he's okay in his skin. His greasy, infected skin.

As the cooks complete their prep work for the day, they begin to work on the more tedious tasks. After a couple of hours, two young ladies come in, with four more men. They are the rest of the back-of-house staff for this shift. Mayra and Eden, the custodial staff, are responsible for vacuuming and cleaning the floors, wiping the windows, cleaning the restrooms, and taking out the trash in the kitchen. All the while they find time for the local *chisme* while rolling silverware.

As the custodial women throw on dirty aprons to get ready for assisting anyone else who may need a helping hand, Meredith saunters into the restaurant. She is a blank emotionless slate and, by the looks of her half-assed makeup and dirty hair, it seems as though her night was hard, but it wasn't. It was just rounded with perplexing thoughts and self-contemplation, nothing abnormal.

Meredith gets settled in. She reads a text from her fiance as she commences her daily work routine. She writes up the seating chart and puts the servers where they go and divides the sections for the day. She doesn't base it on experience; she bases it on how much she likes the server. John, for example, is good at what he does and would be a better manager than herself, but he knows better than to do her job. Since he's the best and knows it (moreover, *Meredith* knows it and is intimidated), he gets a shit section today. Now, Meredith will put someone like Jordan, who's still probably sleeping on the floor of his own bedroom, in a good section. The rest of the staff takes notice that she is constantly giving Jordan special treatment, but she won't discuss Jordan with anyone but Jordan. They have a long and poisonous history. She thinks about this while looking over the liquor count for the week and how different it looks. Charlie is known for doing these orders as carelessly as he can without any penalty.

"This can't be right. Liquor seems way off." she claims.

"You're hungover," he responds. "Don't worry. It's right." He is annoyed, wondering why the fuck some young woman is undermining his ability to count.

"Take a look for yourself. It's gone." Meredith answers back trying to convince him to look.

"Fuck me. Alden's gonna shit himself. Someone must've got in here."

She's off to the back to count the alcohol. The count is wrong. It's a lie, a joke of some sort, she thinks.

She walks by as some more cooks and back of house staff walk in. They are mostly responsible for the final product that is set before the guests. Slowly they all creep to clock in with almost no enthusiasm and much contempt for their employer. They are just shadows that come to do a mindless task and leave when they are done. They have easy hours and work only when they are needed. Just faces in front of a flame; faces in front of the dirty mess caused by both the workers and patrons of Chandler's until it passes onto the next shift. The prep team cuts the garnishes, creates the dressings, and separates the spices to create a signature blend that is only offered at Chandler's.

Outside the frost begins to melt and the workers join together to fight forces of gluttony and greed. Ironically, Sunday tippers are the worst, despite their screams for charity. Most servers will lose money when waiting on churchgoers because they'll leave those fake million dollar bills instead of real bills. At Chandler's, servers will tip two percent of their total sales. So if a server doesn't receive a tip on a table, they still have to pay 2% of that bill to a "tip share" for bussers, hostesses, bartenders, and preps. Just another unfair condition this wait staff works with, which is why on Sundays, most of them walk in somber and lethargic to suffer well.

The wait-staff, hostesses, and bartenders arrive—first Hannah, then Cindy. Some show up together, others straggle in. John, Daniel, Ronald. Jenn, Chelsea, Marty. They check their pens, count their cash and tie their aprons. Aaron's waiting tables today because he needed the extra cash. Maria, Michelle, and Ethan are working doubles today. Ethan is getting closer and closer to his goal with every shift he picks up. Stephanie and Natalie are missing and, of course, Meredith is the one to find them. She wishes she could fire anyone who misses their shift, but they'll just be asked to come in on the next busy shift. If they come in, even if it's three hours late, they'll still have a job and a section.

The staff gets their tables ready with sugars, salt and pepper, new ketchup bottles, and one final wipe down. Chelsea goes into the back to throw her dirty rag in the dirty rag pile. While she's back there she says hello to Juan. They quickly talk about their nights and get ready for a long shift. As she walks away, Juan watches her. He won't get a sight like that for another three hours, minimum. He cherishes the image and it gets him through the day.

Jenn sits at a table, counting her money and loose change, thinking what she should keep on her body to make change for the guests who pay cash. While serving, the staff doesn't have time to go get change out of a register, and working quickly requires one to be ready for anything, including breaking large bills and providing cash customers with exact change. Jenn thinks to herself that if she carries more five dollar bills, customers will be prone to leave her larger bills, which ultimately lead to larger tips. As she's thinking about how to approach her day, she checks her email. Then Vicente approaches her.

"Hey."

Taken by surprise she doesn't know what to do. She smiles up at him and goes back to counting.

"I hear you take pictures now. You do a lot?"

Nervously she responds.

"Yeah. I do."

Knowing who Vicente is, she delicately continues the conversation.

"My brothers and sisters are coming into town soon. Wantin' to know if you could take some pics of us, if it's cool."

"Sure. I could do that. I mean I just started so..."

"Do you charge?"

"I mean..."

"Just lemme know what you charge. I'll take care of you. Find me online. We're friends, no?"

"I think so. I'll message you."

"Cool."

Vicente walks off as quickly as he came in. Alden comes in finally, just right after Jordan. Can't be late if you're walking in with the boss. Alden is wearing his peacoat and his signature red scarf. They nod to each other. His face is smaller than it was yesterday. The workers often argue with one another on whether it's because he's sick or if he's just losing weight. They often speculate to each other about this and pay no attention to their own lives. He tromps quickly to that small closet office. Charlie greets him.

"How's it goin', Alden?"

"Good, good." He responds involuntarily, as if he wasn't listening.

"We're running low on red meats this week. Our seasonings, shortenings, and dry goods are stocked. We need another order for sodas. Fish is good. Liquor, well..."

"What's up?"

"We're running lower than normal. It doesn't match the costs. Meredith caught it this morning."

Alden hangs his coat and scarf. He touches his nose with his index finger as a way of trying to understand what is happening.

"Match like what...someone over-pouring, or someone stealing?"

"Looks like someone's stealin' boss."

"Fuck me! Any idea?"

"Not yet. I'll keep a lookout and review the tapes. After I've made the orders."

"Appreciate it. Just order what you think we need. Let me know if something changes. Fuckin' bullshit. Un*fuckin*believable! Meredith caught this?"

Alden shakes his head no and responds, "Do you want to trust her? Everyone and their mom is friends with that dumb broad. It's more likely to be Dante. I bet it's him, that fuckin' pervert. Lookit, I don't want that shit going down. I'll go out there and tell them about food costs, maybe let 'em know that we're watching and to not fuck around with us. Then the rest is up to them. Idiots will be idiots. They don't listen anyway. I'll probably catch those dumb fucks in the act."

The two men don't speak anymore and look over printed spreadsheets. They are looking over for costs, labor, and other boring things that make the world go round.

Alden goes out to the floor once he's finished. He tells the servers about how the food and liquor costs are out of control and pleads with them to weigh their salads, watch their pours, measure their supplies, and charge extra money for every condiment and side.

Just after, Alden strides to the front of the building and turns on the open sign. He unlocks the door and greets the line waiting at the front with the best attitude and the brightest smile.

VII. Anniversary Date

It's your fourteenth anniversary.

How did you make it this far? You don't know, and quite frankly you're too busy to take the time to put the effort in leaving. You're content with your lifestyle and that is all you really need, or so you think anyway. It's not something you really think about because to *you,* it doesn't matter. Tonight's special. Tonight's the one night you get to remember why you got married in the first place. It's your first time out alone with her in a long time without the obnoxious screams of your children. Your kids are sweet, and sometimes they treat each other with the loving respect that you see on TV sitcoms and single-camera comedies, but the rest of the time they are little shits that you resent.

Your kids are old enough to watch themselves, and though you think they don't *need* a babysitter, you insist that their uncle watches them for the night. Who in their right fucking mind would trust teenage children going through puberty alone in a house with stashed liquor?

Your wife's drinking problem isn't something that bothers you on the surface, but the deep-seeded issues plant themselves every time she sneaks away to her closet. You know it's there, and you want to tell her to simply stop hiding it all together, but you also know that won't matter. It hurts you because your kids see their mother drink herself to sleep almost every night. It would only make matters worse if you actually brought it up. Yet, it breeds secrecy, lies, and contempt. But for tonight, you don't worry about the lies and instead focus on the celebratory excellence of your commitment and hope to get some thick, luscious ass later. Loud and unhinged sex. What you've been needing.

Your wife is giddy with excitement. It's something you both want and maybe she'll remember the good times, too. Like the moment when you first had dinner together at a small fast food fish shop in Dallas. It was all you could afford at the time and neither of you seemed to mind the greasy golden fried shrimp that most likely wasn't real. It really illustrated the kind of woman that she was—someone who didn't really want extravagant things, but would rather have a great cheap date where you could be intimate with one another.

Except now, she wants to go out to another part of Dallas where a beer is eight dollars and you have to pay a cover to get in. You're still too poor to afford shit like that, but better than you were then. Now you support your family of four in a good sixteen hundred square foot house. Food on the plates and cars in the driveway. She pisses you off with her greedy ways, but that's women... or so you think, anyway. In reality, you do love each other very much; there's just been no romance. You've gotten out of touch with your busy lives and you don't eat with each other anymore. She drinks alone and you live a separate life while she stays in isolation in your room.

"Where should we go eat, then?" she asks.

You think it would be good if you go somewhere light, mainstream, and fast. You rationalize this idea by thinking that the less you spend on food, the more money you'll have to spend on drinks, parking, and room service. You decide on a casual restaurant that prides itself in being "home cooked away from home...at its finest," a restaurant that's fairly respectable and big in your city and state. Chandler's. You are good at making choices. Except for the choices you put off.

It's still early, so hopefully you won't have to wait that long, but it appears that rush hour dinner hits hard on a Saturday. The hostess tells you it's a 20-minute wait and assures you that everything is going to be okay and it will most likely take less than that. Her voice seems condescending for a teenager.

What does she know about life?

You and your wife find the only available seat in the waiting area—right by the hostess stand. A beautiful young hostess with the name tag Hannah approaches you, well not you, but the hostess standing next to you. She begins to open her mouth to spill out a river of profanity. You and your wife act like this is shocking but you both know when you were about her age, you were doing far worse things and you always tell yourself that you're thankful social media and picture phones didn't exist when you were growing up. Either way, what young Hannah said you find to be very unprofessional. What child at that age really speaks like this? Why does this

97

turn you away from wanting to do business with Chandler's? You think her parents would be ashamed, and then you wonder if she has parents; but you know she does, just not the good kind. Her parents are probably those who throw money at their kids instead of spending quality time with them. You wish you could give your kids money to shut them the fuck up. Nevertheless, it's none of your business so instead of continuously staring like a creep you look away and grab your wife's hand.

This is nice. You're finally there talking about each other *to* each other. You don't have a lot of time alone with your wife anymore and this makes you sad but up until now, you were unable to vocalize what you miss about the woman you love. You speak so lively that you don't realize the 20-minute mark came and went. Without warning, your wife stands.

"What's taking so long?" she asks in a tone that truly describes how impatient, hungry, and sober she is. "You said it'd be 20 minutes."

Five minutes more go by and no table. You think about going to get a drink at the bar. Maybe a watered-down margarita will help, maybe it won't. You think it mostly won't help because your wife will only nag you about your drinking instead of acknowledging her own. Whatever; you go get one because you deserve one. It's unclear why the table is taking so long to clean up and just as you're about to get your drink you overhear something that Hannah says. You think about it to yourself and you replay it again and again. The words that came out of her mouth. Her sweet. Young. Mouth.

Finally, as you go through the thought again, the buzzer rings and you are taken to a table by a younger, fatter girl with braces. Her ass looks good to you now but you know it'll get bigger as she gets older. Even better, you think. Even better.

As you arrive at your table you see a man standing against a wall just waiting for you to get comfortable and before you can sit he approaches you.

"Hey guys, thanks for coming. Enjoy your meal!" His name tag reads Dante.

Now it clicks in your head, one of the persons Hannah was talking about. The one she was being so *vulgar* about. It creates a sense of concern inside you and just as you really go deep into the thought, your wife reminds you how long it took to get a table in this piece-of-shit restaurant. Your dining experience is just beginning.

Now that you both waited for a table, you get to wait to be fed. And wait some more. And some more. Finally, a young man appears to be approaching your table in a rushed manner. Then he walks right by before you get a chance to lift your arm like a kid at school. You know it's him that's going to be taking care of you. The other one they were talking about at the hostess stand. This is going to be one hell of an experience. You caught the name tag on him and know you're screwed.

"I apologize. I'll be right back with you," says the young man. You are already thinking that it's going to be a long while before he comes back. He appears to be more concerned with something other than his tables. You can see it in his face and you can tell because of his balance and his clumsy walk. There is a way you can validate your presumptions about Jordan but you don't wish to indulge in his storyline yet. "Can we just get a couple of waters while we wait?"

"Sure. Give me a moment."

Your wife is annoyed. Her tone gives it away and if it's not fixed soon, it could mean trouble for your special night. The waiter walks off and doesn't come back for a few minutes. When he returns, he does so with great enthusiasm...

"Hi y'all, I'm Jordan and I'll be taking care of you. Would you like to start off with an ice cold beer or one of our frozen margarita specials?"

With his name uttered you realize now how screwed you really are. He is the one. The other guy those little girls in the front spoke so poorly of. The one that

Hannah talked about and made fun of to her other little friends. The exact details, though not authenticated, were enough to give your wife an uneasy tension. Enough so, that she will make sure that Jordan has a hard time working your table this evening.

"You never brought us our waters…"

You remember waiting tables back in the day. It was different when everything wasn't computerized and digitized. You had to pull your own weight and you sure as shit had to know how to handle 12 table sections. Back in your glory day, filled with passionate ambition and vitality. You can empathize. You did that. You've been there, desperate for attention, money, and meaning. Not anymore though, as this anniversary is proof of that. But now you remember how much better it is to be the person *at* the table instead of the one standing *above* it.

You don't step in and you let your wife do the dirty talk for you. You like it when she gets dirty. Just like at home. Raw and unfiltered with her emotions and with her wants and needs. She's a type of gal that was never afraid to speak her mind. Something you always found sexy about her. The commanding presence she walks with turns you on and is one of the reasons why you are here tonight with this woman. You sometimes forget this and it's sad that you do.

Out of nowhere a busser brings your waters. Now
Jordan asks if you're ready. Remembering where food
comes from, and from watching way too many Netflix
documentaries about poor food handling, you try to find
something that can't be screwed or skewed with and
order something that resembles chicken and vegetables.
Your wife goes with a more colorful plate that mocks
other foods and cultures, the type of dish that claims to
be this or that but is rather something invented in a
marketing scheme to attract more diversity and taste to a
restaurant. Some fusion dishes like those made-up egg
rolls with a southern Texas twist: Italian Sausage Burger
Quesadillas. *Who the fuck creates that? That must taste
like shit.* You despise fusion dishes. Before the waiter
runs off, both you and your wife order two different
alcoholic drinks. As Jordan walks off, he says something
he thinks that you couldn't hear. You and your wife
heard it perfectly. Now she's pissed off, which makes you
upset. You feed too much on other people's emotions
and have a tendency to take to heart what someone else
is feeling. You don't even have to know a person but if
you saw a stranger crying, you'd cry along with them.
Like you carry the pain of the world on your shoulders.
As your order is getting fulfilled, your wife becomes
more impatient and asks you some questions about why

you came to this decision to eat here. You can't defend yourself anymore so you make up some excuses.

"Normally this place isn't so busy. It's usually good here. Must be that rush. Doesn't matter because we have the whole night."

It's loud and you have to speak louder to get your words across. Drunk laughter echoes throughout the freshly painted walls. Children screaming for more food vibrates your table and kitchen sounds and screams can be heard around the corner.

Remember working at a restaurant so many years ago? You helped pay your way through college when it wasn't so expensive. You could make friends anywhere you went—with coworkers and customers alike. Back when customers appreciated that, anyway. Do they still appreciate that? You don't think they do, but you remember that people will always be defined in a restaurant: both sitting at the table and waiting on it. The good people treat each other like kings. The bad people treat each other worse.

You sit in an awkward silence and stare at your wife as she checks her phone without once glancing up. You try to remember why you fell for her to begin with and what has kept you both together for so long. Maybe because you used to hate yourself so much that anyone who gave you affection was worthy of your life, love, and soul.

Then you realized that she is just like you. You're best friends. You know each other in and out, your dislikes and your likes. She was there for you when you were picking up shifts while you went to school. You were there for her whenever she needed you to be. And though it may not seem like it, you *know* you deeply care. You cared enough to come this far and you care enough to go further. She has a homely face, nothing over the top, but what she lacks in looks she makes up in other sexual areas. You think that's probably the alcohol in her body when she does engage you in intimacy. Her body is what you enjoy and you like the way her body feels—especially when you compare it to those past "hardbody" types. Women with too much muscle made for some horrible sex partners and also made you feel so self-conscious. If only this experience could show it. Saturday nights at Chandler's isn't the most ideal spot to reignite a fizzling romance. It's getting later and later and no drinks come by. Jordan is sitting at the bar. You have straight sight of him. He's just sitting there waiting with his hands crossed at his mouth. He looks over at you and nods.

"Sorry I'm just waiting on your drinks. This bartender sucks. He takes *forever.*"

You're looking right at your drinks. Why doesn't this guy just pick them up and bring them over? What the fuck is going through that guy's head? Seriously! You see Jordan carelessly pick a cherry out of a jar and take a bite. He notices the drinks in front of his block head are in fact the drinks you and your wife ordered. He picks them up in a rush and as he does the jar of cherries spill over and lands on the floor. It's everywhere! The spill is beginning to spread and consume the dry tile by the bar. "Oops," you see him mouth to himself. Oops?! That's all. He says he'll get it cleaned up and walks away. This guy is an idiot. He doesn't do anything he is supposed to. When there is a spill you stay put until someone can clean it up. It's a dim-lit restaurant and not everyone can see the dark red liquid across the dark brown tile.

Before you can finish your thought about what you know about safety procedures, a young girl slips with a tray full of glasses in her hand. The cups tumble on each other and crash slowly on the tray and then onto her face. She hits her head on the floor and a concoction of soft drinks and syrup swirl around her fallen body.

Your wife turns her head in disbelief. "Oh my god!"

You go and help the poor girl out. You apologize and get the name off her tag. Jenn, a woman that carries herself with too much pride to be bothered by such a mishap. A busser comes with towels, a dingy mop, and a faded wet floor sign. A woman in a business casual outfit comes by and says to not worry about it. She helps the girl to her feet while instructing the young busser to clean the mop before he places it on the ground and to get fresh water.

Confused, she asks what happened. You tell her everything you saw and she acts like she understands and walks off.

You just want to fucking eat at this point. Apparently that's a lot to ask for in a goddamn restaurant. That cheap fish joint in Dallas sounds good right about now, except it's probably not there anymore.

Jordan disappeared and hasn't been seen since the big spill. You don't know it but his friend, the woman in the business casual outfit you told the story to, is trying to search for him to discuss the idea about how he can avoid losing his job today. You excuse yourself to the restroom to wash up and just before you make your way back, you spot them at the entrance of the back of house.

"What do you think you're *doing*?" It's all you really hear. It is hard to make out exactly what they are saying to each other but you notice the woman is attempting to be firm and real with Jordan, but Jordan seems complacent. He looks slightly pissed off but more so; he looks sad and disappointed, but not about his actions, about *her* actions.

When you return to your table, after all of that commotion, your food comes in. Your wife is still on her phone and takes a picture of her plate. She takes a picture of you and your plate too. You question her methodology because just a moment ago she was complaining about how her blood sugar was low.

The food arrives and it looks good. The veggies look fresh and the chicken breast has perfectly cross grill marks on it. You take your first bite...and the food is cold! That's the problem with these "home cooked" kinds of places. Everything is precooked in the morning and then reheated in the evening for people like you. Except not heated up for people like you. You remember from experience that this is nothing personal: when people in the back of the restaurant are screaming for food there is always that one person out of several hundreds or even thousands of guests that will get screwed over and have a bad experience. You are that one person. Today it's *your* day to get screwed. You look around to see if anyone else is showing signs of anger, and they are not. Everyone else is happy, laughing and shoveling food in their jolly fucking faces.

You wait for Jordan to come back into your life but time keeps passing on. Your drink and your wife's drink just sit there. Half empty. Then your wife begins to express that you have a look on your face that she seldom sees. It's the face of stress, anger, hunger, the extreme displeasure, the bullshit irritation. You ramble to her.

"This is stupid. I can't believe this. This *would* happen to us on a night like this."

"Don't be dramatic."

"That spill by the bar was pretty dramatic."

"I don't even want to deal with them. You can have some of my food if you like."

"I'll take some."

You eat, disappointed.

"It's busy, I know it. But they should be able to do their job." You say this as you eat your wife's food that you continuously criticize in your head.

Your wife nods her head in agreement.

The waiter finally comes back and just as the anger is festering inside, before you could even gather your words...

"Hey guys I'm sorry about all that. How's your food? Sucks? Oh man, I'm sorry. Yea, this place sucks. I'm not going to be here much longer. I can't stand it here. I'm sorry. I just feel bad because this place really does suck. I'll see what I can do about your food. I'll get you some hookups. Don't worry. Maybe I'll get the manager to take care of your food."

He never really addresses that he is the problem but points the blame on the establishment. You know better than that. You know that there is no such thing as an establishment. There is no magical person pulling all of the strings because unlike him, *you* have complete control of your life. Your failures are your own, and once you realize that, your quality of life improves substantially.

You remember what the hostess said earlier and deep down you know that everything in his life is his own fault. *Entirely.* You know better, because at one point you were the same way. You say out loud:

"Nobody likes you. I don't. The hostesses don't. Your manager only puts up with you because you have two legs that can walk. You're just a blank slate. Get me your manager."

Jordan's face turns red. His grimace transforms into something dark. "I'm sorry, what was that?"

You sit and smirk.

"He said to get your manager," your wife repeats triumphantly, as if she was a prosecutor that won an infamous murder trial.

Jordan stands there dumbfounded. You hold your glare. Another manager walks by. He is dressed up wearing a peacoat and red scarf. He was on his way out but notices your skirmish.

"Is everything okay?"

"We just need some warm food and a different server. We'd hate for you to lose our business over something so silly."

He is stalled in disbelief. He wants you to start from the top and tells Jordan to go away. He gets your long-winded story. All of it. Even the bit about your anniversary. He calls John over, a much more glorious man with a handsome face and a comforting smile. He is ready to please both you and your wife to a delicate treat. Eager to show you how much better he is than what's-his-face. That smile makes you forget about the horrendous crimes against your dinner.

Both you and your wife are content. Alden, the general manager, gets you more than you could ask for, including a gift card. He also tells you to ask for him whenever they dine in so he can personally check and make sure you're enjoying yourselves. The rest of your meal is perfect. You don't forget about Jordan, but you don't care about what will happen to him. He's not your problem. While they prepare you fresh food, Alden brings you another appetizer on the house so you don't starve. John is much more pleasant. He's homely. Like you used to be. Like you still are. While your dinner is getting recooked and paid for by the house, you get to tell your wife that she looks beautiful in your eyes. You get to really talk about the last five years and where they went. Dinner to you is couples therapy. It's your time to truly connect with someone. "Table talk" is what you call it. Your table talk is going so well that you've decided to talk the talk and walk the walk. Even though your dinner is done, your night has just begun.

The Lunch Special

Not everyone that works and eats in a restaurant is an addict. In fact there are several "normal" people who come in to do their job and go home. Several of them don't want to tell their story or even want their story to be told.

Ronald

I'm here to help my wife pay for medical school because that shit isn't cheap. I want her to really just live her dream out and if that means working two jobs, then so be it. Once she's done and working, she's going to give me the same privilege of going back to school. I want to go back and get my Masters degree so I can become an administrator in education. It's corny but I want to clean up the school system.

111

Marty

I honestly don't know how any of those bitches work high and drunk all the time. When I drink, all I want to do is nap. When I get high, all I want to do is nap. When I clock in all I want to do is nap. I wouldn't be much use. I guess it just depends on the person.

Aaron

It's the easiest way to make money besides selling cars. Fuck selling cars.

Maria

I'm going to school and it helps pay the bills. I'm studying to be a teacher. Elementary school. I'm about to start my student teaching. Once that begins, I'll *still* have to work here during the nights because they won't pay me. I've worked here for over four years, ever since I got out of high school.

Michelle

I used to be a stripper. The money isn't as good here, but it's more honest than taking off your clothes for thirsty married men. I'm going to get baptized soon!

Ethan

I work two jobs, too. This is for extra cash to pay off all my bullshit credit cards I took out when I was a young idiot. Two more weeks of this shit and I will have enough to completely pay my debt. After, I'm going to get the fuck out of here. I have plans.

Andrea

Do I like it here? It's okay. Better than most places I've worked at. I do like the sense of community here. Between the workers and the guests. I do have a side gig of course—I do some videos and modeling on the side. I want to get to New York City. I also dance, too! I have tryouts for my college coming up soon. I'll be out of here this month. Maybe I'll be able to wait tables in the big apple. Did you hear about Jordan and Meredith?

Cindy

I'm just an ol' angry bitch that works here. Now fuck off.

Mayra

[Translated from Spanish]

Why does anyone work? To support yourself! To support your family and pay for the roof over your head and the food on the table. God can only give me so much, I have to work for the rest. I'm setting a good example for my children that hard work will pay off.

Eden
Yes. I work here. It's okay.

Family of Six
No, I wouldn't say we normally come here. Maybe once a month? Not exactly sure. The chicken tenders are really good. My four kids really enjoy them. You get a lot of bang for your buck here and the kids like going out to eat. Plus me and the husband don't have to clean up their dishes. That's exhausting. What do I like? I'm not really partial to one thing. I like the beer-battered fried shrimp and my husband always likes a good deal on ribeye. Wait, who are you again?

Young Love
-This place is amazing!

-We love this place!

-We can afford it, the people are cool. I go to school with a lot of them.

-Yeah, it's nice to see our friends.

-Don't tell anyone but they hook us up with free stuff too!

-Yeah, our friend Hannah likes to give us some shakes and drinks for free. She'll text us when it's cool to come by and sneak us some drinks too! She told me to apply here and use her as a reference. Says the guys are always giving her things.

-Hell yeah!

Sharon the Bar Regular

Meredith is my regular at the bar. She comes in a lot to see me and this is me just returning the favor. We met at one of our first jobs together and stayed in touch. I give her drinks, she gives me food!

VIII. Thanks for the Tip

It seems like John will be working as a server for the rest of his life. Even after he dies, he thinks that he'll suffer unfairly for some sins he didn't understand and be condemned to serve demons in hell. How fitting that would be for him. He despises his job every day that he comes in except for Tuesdays. He actually looks forward to working on Tuesdays. Working in the same place for such a long time has its perks. John opened the location about 10 years ago and since he's lasted this long, he's the most trusted employee: he gets first call on his schedule, and a never ending supply of regulars that

115

keeps his pockets more packed than anyone else's at Chandler's.

Laura is a recent regular by only a few months and she often comes in at the same time every Tuesday. Really, she's not the most beautiful girl in the world, but she is to John. It's tragic that she comes to eat alone. John wonders why she's always alone and why such a beautiful person would be alone, but frankly it's because nobody shares the same eyes. Laura's wide set eyes and narrow nose fit perfectly together, and in John's perspective those features work well, though compared to conventional beauty standards, she wouldn't be seen as attractive. Jordan and Dante don't see the unique features as something that's special. John thinks she's new to town or recently single. Maybe her friends are back stabbers and she's starting a new life. John questions this every time he sees her and comes up with deep narratives for her. The imagination of why; why her, why here, and why alone? Yet, for whatever reason, he's never had the courage to dive too deep into conversation. John's really afraid of revealing himself to her and scared of showing off how imperfect his life is, especially to someone he fancies. Every Tuesday night she's dressed up in her heels, with her glasses and hair naturally doing its own curl. The same drink and the same dinner: a rum and cola, the grilled catfish with mashed potatoes and broccoli. Always in the same booth by the bar. Always the same, never a change. A true creature of habit.

John never gets tired of her and he always takes very good care of her. He treats her like royalty; not in an ironic way, but because he truly sees her as a queen. He gives her service like a queen. Every type of meeting between them reminds him that he could be doing better with himself. Her job, her outfit, the way she reads a different book every time she comes in. He thinks he doesn't have the time to read but wishes he did. John will have Laura summarize the stories for him and ask her what she thinks of them. She, in turn, answers and goes on to say why it's important to know other stories.

"You really should pick up one of these yourself." she starts. "I think it's vital. It's important to read these stories because it creates a deeper understanding of who we are as people. It creates tolerance, it creates sympathy, and it can even give you a new perspective. I think if people would read more, there would be less hate in the world. It's sad though, that we still have to teach so many people in the working world how to read."

Johns knows this to be true. He knows that most of the servers he works with don't read, nor do they bother. Realistically, they just follow the masses in substanceless, mindless scrolling on their devices. His opinion on this matter is not true, but being the self-centered man he is, he believes himself to be better than his coworkers. He enjoys her conversation and her intelligence. He looks forward to Tuesday nights because he knows he'll get taught something he never wanted to know otherwise. One week she was reading a book about an older Jewish man. In this story, the man wrote a book for his lost love that was separated from him during the Holocaust but was later reunited with his estranged son. Another week she told him the story of *Dorian Gray*. He was learning to understand a new voice every week.

There is a true commitment between the two, well, as much commitment that there can be between a server and their guest. If John doesn't come in, she won't eat there and if she doesn't come in, John will have a horrible night thinking about his missed connection.

Most people gravitate towards John and his great attitude, but nobody knows the battle that exists inside his own brain. He hides it well, the way he carries himself to and from work with such pride and strength. It is more than alluring. He is vocal about how he hates his job, but he is also too arrogant to show his pain. He is too nice to hurt anyone and that's his weakness. He's tall and handsome, but in a nerdy Ross-from-*Friends* kind of way, with his wild hair and professor-like fashions. John himself believes that he does have a higher purpose; he just hasn't figured it out yet. Laura likes this about John, knowing that he holds infinite possibilities. He can do whatever he wants because he's not tied to anyone or anything.

Anything except for this encounter once a week.

Laura, in her mid-20s, sits so graciously with her legs crossed. She sits in silence observing the customers, workers, and scenery of Chandler's. Laura looks forward to their meeting every Tuesday. She is a professional and carries herself as an extremely confident strong woman who can get what she wants, when she wants it. She never made it clear to John what she does, but she was one of the lucky ones that got out of college and found a real nice paying job. John wonders how the hell she did it. Nepotism perhaps? Unfortunately, he knows in his cynical brain that other professional industries can be sexist, but she has not fallen victim to this trend. It's in her smile; it's a smirk that's not completely centered or symmetrical but perfectly fit for her big brown eyes.

It can make a man swoon.

It seemed like a chance that they would meet again in the same spot week after week, but it was so meticulously planned by Laura. She can put together the schedule in her mind. Tonight, she is especially excited to come in, with hopes that he will be forward with her. She even planned on which story to tell him. A contemporary

119

classic told in second person, one that takes place in
New York, about a man who works in the Department
of Factual Verification. She tells John that her days at
work are getting better and better. She smiles with him,
and flirts with him when she feels good about herself.
John understands body language. Very much so. His
years of service to the fortunate masses keeps him sharp
for his tables. He quickly catches on but instead of
playing against the tide of her good nature, he simply
plays with her and reigns as enigmatic as he possibly can
be. She understands what he's doing and she loves it.
She can't be fooled but neither can he. Two very witty
people dropping hints in an infinite loop. Neither one of
them wants to give in and their stubbornness may keep
them in that loop.

"I understand, do you?"

"Yes, I do. You think you're smart?"

"I know I am. I know what you're doing."

"Well if you know it, then what am I doing?"

Their conversation is redundant, but that is the
epitome of human nature. By the time the opportunity is
gone and then the world becomes tedious. The mind
goes elsewhere to something, or someone to fill that
void.

Every Tuesday the time passes, and not a single move
out of the other, even though the hints are so obvious.

With time running out for each other, the mediocrity of their lives tugs at the corner of her blouse. By this time next week she could find a man suitable for her needs. Maybe a man that's too confident. She'll settle on someone who doesn't fit her needs, but makes her feel desired. Not one that exceeds her expectations, just one that meets them. How boring.

Then he'll rethink it over and over to himself. *What if?* Life never begins with a question. The sooner they figure that out, the better.

The first drink comes so quickly, and by the time it comes, they have already wasted so much time flirting with their own demise. Before John has a moment to greet her with his smile and stories, her food is ready and in another instant the check is printed and placed in front of her. Now all she needs to do is sign the credit card slip with her tip and to get in her car and go home, off into the night. Her dinner is over in the blink of an eye.

Ceremonies like this don't last long, but there are life-lasting implications. Nobody is certain they are destined for each other, but they won't know if they don't, at least, attempt to find out.

To any outsider it's obvious to say that those two, John and Laura, feel something for each other. The way she comes in through the entryway, and the way Hannah

sees her with a big smile, knowing exactly where to seat
her and why. The way the bartender sees her sit in the
booth. And when she leaves, everyone is let down. John
is constantly thinking about her and yet, he never moves
in for the kill. When it's the end of the night, John
always thinks he'll get the balls to ask her on a date, but
she's already gone.

Laura leaves and John is full of regret. John lets her
leave and Laura is disappointed. The only thing John is
left with is the signature and 20 percent tip written on this
receipt. She doesn't leave a message. His subtle
tightening of his mouth expresses so much frustration
with himself, but maybe he'll see her next week. Maybe
he'll have another chance.

Laura drives off and begins to listen to 90s rock and
pop on her phone. She checks her phone three times,
and each time with nothing on it. No messages, no
missed calls, no voicemails, no emails. She tosses it
carelessly on the empty seat next to her. She turns the
volume up on her car and places her left hand on her
forehead. She is angry with herself and the actions of
John, or rather John's lack of actions. No initiative.
Maybe he's not interested, or maybe she doesn't know
how to show how *she's* interested. She has this thought
in her head that she can't seem to get over. The law that
states a man must initiate the relationship. The law of the

commercialized world of magazines that make women feel like shit for not wearing makeup even though a woman like Laura doesn't need it with her flawless skin.

Why didn't he get my number, my contact info, my business card, my email, my anything?! Better yet, why didn't I give him that info?! She questions herself and begins to doubt everything that she does with lasting implications.

Oh well, she thinks to herself. Now she begins to realize the opportunities in front of her. She thinks hard and then remembers a man she works with. Someone who is throwing himself at her. Her angered face turns to relief. It's not too late to show him that there could be something between them. He's a nice guy. He's not bad looking and he has a better job than this John guy.

Meanwhile back at Chandler's, John studies her signature. Laura Martinez.

All of the confidence left him when her purse left that table. Table 12. The corner booth. It sits with her crumbs and her drink's condensation. As he busses her table he tries to remember everything that went on. He tries to justify why he didn't make the move. He tries to realize he could've made the move long ago. He looks back at how different the night could have gone.

He remembers when she first came to the restaurant. One year ago. She was lively and as beautiful as she is now. John didn't think anything of it then but now it seems like he is about to lose someone very important.

Now John is left here alone hoping it won't be too late. It seems difficult to him because he can't understand what he is feeling. Finally it clicks. It's simply because it's something he's never felt before. He's in love. He wishes he would've recognized it sooner. But what would a successful lady like her do with a guy like him? He goes into the kitchen and begins cleaning up the mess of the staff. His workers silently polish the stainless steel. They then exchange how much they made. While the energetic few go home with lots of cash, some go home empty handed and in tears. John goes home alone. More alone than ever.

He thinks to himself. The next time he sees her she won't be alone. He honestly believes that he'll have lost his chance. But, if she *is* alone, and she does step through that door again, he'll have the confidence needed to go after what he wants. He could've done that a long time ago but he didn't. He too doubts himself. He questions why he does things the way he does. This was a wake-up call. Next time he sees her, he's going to go for it. He won't care if she's with someone. He'll have what it takes. He goes home to try to make sense of it.

Before the servers either pass out or wake up, John is alone dreaming. Laying down in a couple of sheets and a horrible excuse for a bed, John envisions a restaurant with lost souls and no efficiency. He is trapped in an endless shift of waiting tables. With faceless patrons coming to eat one by one, John is the only one there to completely take care of all aspects of his work. This includes, but is not limited to, seating, bussing, serving, prepping, and even in some cases, cooking. The ghosts continue to order and progressively get more and more pissed off. John is in the weeds and he can't find his way out. He can't catch up; every time one problem arises, another shortly comes to irk his straight and calm mindset. Someone is waiting on their check, someone else is waiting for their drink, someone waits for their food. Everyone is looking at him, asking him what's the wait. *What is the wait? What's taking you so long, John? You're normally good at this.*

Every task he finishes, two more blindside him and take away from the other three that were on his mind. John continues to get overwhelmed. He takes a breath and walks slowly but it never goes away. One problem after another until it is too late. John begins to have a panic attack. John begins to shake while he shrinks to the size of a beer bottle. The guests of his begin to grow larger and larger, until he is chased. Now he's too small to handle the issue. He's too small to do anything. Then he wakes up and realizes that this dream is symbolic to

125

his simple idle boring life. The worst part about this nightmare is that it will still be there when he wakes up.

* * *

On the next lonely Tuesday night after John went through an insufferable week filled with drugs, rape, illness, and death, Laura walks in the door. John notices her immediately and can't wait to vent to her about all the bullshit that went on. He approaches her like never before. He's relieved she's not with anyone and no longer berates himself, but with his attitude, if she did walk in with a guy, he would've found a way to get rid of him. John, as always, is captivated by her gentleness and intelligence and right before she is seated, John takes her hand, a very bold move that surprises everyone including himself, and looks at her in her eyes. A look similar to one as if he's completed a marathon: proud.

With the biggest smile he has he looks into her brown eyes and asks a very simple question after a quick hello.

"How are you this evening?" He waits for her to answer.

"You're not going to take my drink order?" She blushes and becomes red as the excitement fills her head.

"Laura, you know what? You've been coming in here for a long while, now. I feel like I don't really know you that well. Yet. Can we go to a more...hmm, the words escape me..."

Laura seems pleased and lets him finish the sentence.

"Can we go somewhere more appropriate for a conversation like this."

Without skipping a beat he laughs. Perhaps if he did this earlier in their meeting it wouldn't have meant this much.

"When do you get off?" she asks him, calmly looking for an answer. She can tell he's troubled. John's eyes begin to swell. The rush of emotions commands his involuntary ability to hold back his pain. He looks around. He watches Dante sitting at the bar laughing at probably some stupid ass dick joke. Jordan is standing by the restrooms texting someone. Everyone else is faking it. There is no real emotion here; the people that eat here are completely unaware of how the world is dying right before them. But Laura is. He comes to the conclusion very quickly in his mind that Chandler's is full of shit-faced people filled with shit. Seeing her face and hearing these stories she's told him reminds him that he's not doing anything. He's just a simple-minded person working the motions.

"Now. I get off now."

His answer astounds her. He walks out with everything.

There is a small pause. It happened so quickly but so smoothly. She was almost caught by surprise but halfway expected it. Of course what she didn't expect was for him to leave his post so purposefully. John realizes it's time to wake up from this dream. He walks to Dante and takes off his apron and calmly places it right in front of him. Dante doesn't try to keep him. He doesn't try to change his mind but allows him to walk away to freedom. John escorts Laura to the front of the building and walks outside. He places his foot on the bench to tie his shoe and looks up at Laura, his new opportunity.

"Where do you want to go?" John asks.

"Well, I was going to eat here. I guess that's out of the question now."

IX. Take Out

She wakes up late and hears all the names she's been called since she started working at Chandler's: slut, broad, bitch, ho, whore, and nothing. Nothing. That one hurts the most. Jenn does everything she can to become something—*anything*—but when the sting comes it still hurts and it hurts bad. She wants to blame her mother for always derailing her from her dreams and beating the shit out of her self-esteem. That stupid bitch. She'd say things to eat at her self-worth and make what's left of her ego rot away.

You'll never be a good mother if all you do is write. You can't make a living in music. You can't do shit with an art degree. Teachers aren't respectable in this society.

She doesn't necessarily believe that to be true, but every time her mother opens her ugly mouth, Jenn would change her major in hopes it will mean something to her mother.

Jenn wants to be lots of things: a reporter, a writer, a video producer, an editor, a musician, a photographer, a teacher, and of course she wants to do work for a non-profit, something that makes a difference in the world around her. Unfortunately, she listened to everyone's discouraging words and slander and decided to go against everything she believes in. She does this almost every day before she lifts her head from her pillow. She is a server and a bartender working as much as she can so she can afford to dream about what happens next. She dropped out of college in spite of how much talent she had. This was a young girl that would receive great accolades for her skills at the trombone. It's a random instrument for a short girl but she could move that slide with ease and vigor. She joined one of the best music schools in the nation and was on her way.

Now she's left with her rotten mother, helping pay bills that are not her responsibility. One more resentment to the pile that's been building up since she was six years old and taken out of ballet class. While in high school she had to work and juggle her schedule with marching band and being a closing hostess. Wake up, then school from 7:30–2:30, band practice every day from 3–5, then work from 6–11. That did not include the football games and competitions she was required to attend. She gave up her student life to be an adult. She lived to please the only grown-up in her life. Her damaged self-esteem would cause her to go for ugly stupid boys, drop out of a good school, and not finish anything because of her paralyzing fear of failure.

Jenn still finds herself jealous of some of her coworkers, especially the young girls like Hannah. They all have cars, big ass houses, looks, parties, and not a care in the world. Jenn has an overbearing and over-judgemental mother, a small apartment, and a student career she left behind. She's also got a boyfriend, Lance. The one that was handsome and seemed so encouraging at first, but then slowly showed his ugly, impatient side when she would begin a conversation about her passions.

Most days, Lance just stares blankly and confused as she enthusiastically shares her dreams and desires. The look of disappointment that she didn't follow along in the American Dream: where you work to death for nothing but an ideal. Ideals are meant to be something more. Working long hours and not having time for herself is not Jenn's idea of an American dream. She feels alone because who at her job wants to listen to her rant about Trombone Shorty or Christian Lindberg? She'll pull shit out of her ass and enthusiastically quote Thorton Wilder, Oscar Wilde, Arthur Miller, and Simon Stephens. Even Irvine Welsh isn't fun enough to keep her boy toy's interest. Bukowski? Nobody around her seems to give a shit about any of it. Not because they're stupid or because they're not educated enough, or because they don't care to read; it's the bullshit lifestyle that they are living. She forgets that these co-workers of hers are working to live and can't spare the time to read a book when some don't even know if their water will be on when they get home. Or if the custody of their children will rule in their favor. The job at Chandler's makes all the staff forget about self-care. That's why so many of them are addicted to some type of substance. For Jenn, her addictions are sex, music and art. Self-validating through her boyfriend's hard cock and some indie bullshit she heard on YouTube or SoundCloud. Unfortunately, she's finding it hard to get off with Lance's growing condition.

Lance started looking like shit about a year ago and is getting uglier by the day. Maybe it's the free chicken tenders, the unlimited bread and soda, or the number of beers he drinks, but something is tearing this once handsome boy apart. What used to be a ripped man wrapped in ink has since stretched out his own tattoos. In bed, Jenn still envisions him in his prime, but it only gets her off for a while and never the time that she needs. To her, the handsome and fit Lance still is the one who pokes at her when they're laying in bed together. She remembers days when he was interested in who she was.

When they first met Lance would offer to stay with her as she finished her side work and then they would stay long after the restaurant closed to talk. Soon they would flirt, kiss and then they would be feeling up on each other in a wonderful way. With their faces orange by the parking lights, She'd tell him everything she thought and he would hang onto every word.

Turns out he was listening just so he could get laid, as Jenn was too good for him. She would have to go down to his level to put up with him for just a little while longer.

Lance has taken a great interest in video games but Jenn isn't as fascinated by it. Instead of working on her craft as an artist, she'll smoke, drink, or take a pill if she can score one off of Vicente. She blames Lance for her

new vices but all they do is go to work, go to the
Graveyard, and then go home to play video games.
While he gets online, Jenn just sits there—bored—longing
for the days when she actually felt accomplished and
proud of something. But the truth is she's never really
felt that way. Definitely not proud of anything. How
could she feel proud of herself when everyone in her life
was disappointed by her? Even at work she'd put up with
the bullshit. But her being sedated came at an advantage
to Lance, for he was looking for a quick lay that'd last as
long as his debilitated libido would allow, which is now
down to about 36 seconds. That's 20 seconds shorter
than last month. At this point, she is desperate enough to
accept any type of attention he'll give to her. She's having
a quarter-life crisis.

She knows where her next meal is coming from. She
knows how to "feel good," and this is what her life will be
like. They'll get married and repeat the process until they
die. At this point in her short life she doesn't have any
more ambitions beyond getting to bed. Day after day,
with a never ending river of alcohol and never ending
passion. That's what Lance calls it. Passion. It's all
routine and so what if she's bored?

The end.

Except...

Lance wasn't going to fuck the life out of Jenn anymore. She doesn't care for him like she used to but she doesn't have the confidence to do anything about it. Yet, she can hear a voice in her head screaming at her to chase her dreams, dump this loser and change her life. Her dreams are beginning to yell at her to let them out. Sometimes dreams can get lost in infatuation.

They came back to her slowly but it wasn't until she heard about a poor girl who killed herself that she began to acknowledge what she was doing to herself.

It was all anyone could talk about with their politically correct bullshit and up until now, Jenn considered doing it to herself. Jenn didn't want to kill herself but she didn't want to live either. She almost gave up and didn't care if she was slowly killing herself with Lance, alcohol, and other paraphernalia. Maybe then, she wouldn't be cursed to hell. That's her way of thinking, but then the thought left her as fast as it came. Suddenly she's back in reality getting her drinks from the bar and she slips.

Now she's on the floor hurt and embarrassed because of Jordan's carelessness. Her boyfriend is hysterically laughing at her fall.

As a customer helps her up on her feet, she screams at Lance.

"Why the fuck are you laughing at me? You're supposed to be helping me you dick!"

She knows she will not get through to him, but she yells it anyway. This is the first time she's confronted Lance about anything. Lance, now speechless and realizes that in all the span of their relationship, the only way he knew how to comfort her was pointing his hard prick in her face.

She runs into the kitchen and into the dry storage—the area where most servers go to cry. As her hair leaks with a mixture of beer and soda, she thinks about the girl she found out about on the news. It was her. The one she was in the school band with. Jenn thinks of her but she can't get over the fact that perhaps if she was a more assertive person, she could've prevented this from happening. Death can creep up on a person fast and Jenn knows if she were to die right now, her last moment on Earth would've been an embarrassing one.

Now she knows and can see that the only way her boyfriend can comfort her with is his hard cock. She cries to herself in a room full of spices, sauces, rice, beans and nuts about her lack of a support system. She needs to get home and fortunately, Dante doesn't want this incident on his shift summary and definitely doesn't want to get sued.

She comes home and while she waits for Lance, she begins to get nauseous. She can't seem to figure out why she's getting sick. She thinks about the food, she thinks about drinking, maybe the drugs. No matter what she does, she always ends up sick to her stomach or on the toilet. She can't go to the doctor because she doesn't have insurance and that would waste time and money. It's bullshit to think that these profitable restaurants have yet to figure out how to take care of their employees. She wanted to take a trip to the doctor before but every time her prince Lance would whine and stop her from going. She recalls going once and then being yelled at for not having the money to stay out for a few more drinks, or enough to buy a 12 pack. That's what matters. At least he'd have his video games to keep him sedated for the evening. She's expecting too much.

He gets home. Opens the door, pissed off.

"Sick!" he yells. "That's a good hundred bucks you missed today!"

She looks at him and sadly she remembers her mother, her peers, and all the projects and schooling she'd never finish. Sick. That's why she's been going home every day. She thinks about telling him that something may be wrong with her. Instead the shame she's built inside her head is too much. She apologizes and goes into the room to sleep it off.

Not good enough. Tomorrow she has to go to work again to make what money she can, and to greet her guests with a smile like nothing's wrong. None of her customers want to hear about Lindburg, Wilde, Wilder, Stephens, or her manic depression. She even hears her mother telling her what she believes is true.

She holds the pillow in her arms. Fuck that, what does she know? Who does she think she is? She has her problems too. Fuck that. Fuck Lance, too. What has he done that's of any actual help for her? When the fuck did she become so dependant on other people's approval? This thought lasts until the morning.

She's at work and realizes that her job is literally based on how people judge her. How they perceive her motions, her nuances in picking up menus off the table. How elegant can someone be when refilling an ice-cold sweet tea? How good a woman is at remembering four meals to ring up in the system. How will the guests perceive her when she mistakenly gives a customer a Coke when in fact they ordered a Diet Coke? Or when she switches the meals when bringing them out? They will judge the shit out of her. They will take money away from her tip and chastise the fuck out of Jenn, or they won't. They won't notice and their ideas of what money they put in Jenn's pocket won't change. Jenn thinks of this while most of her co-workers don't. John might think this way. Isabel, too. Maybe Daniel has this crazy neurotic side to him. Lance doesn't. He can't see anything nor does he care about anything. Jenn is slowly coming to the realization that she is completely envious of that trait.

She gets to work and is thrown off by how busy the restaurant is. Lance is stressed in the parking lot and Jenn is annoyed with the number of cars piled up. Whenever a server can't find a parking spot, it's a good indication that the shift is going to start off by cleaning up the mess from lunch. When they walk in they are both put in the middle of the heat and asked to pick up tables immediately. Isabel screams at them over the patron chatter and the '80s hits playing on the radio.

"Oh thank God you're here! I thought I was going to have to wait till 10 after to start giving tables up. Look, there is a four-top ready to order, I already got them their drinks. Another two-top over at 91; they haven't been greeted yet, and there is a six-top over in the bar. I have their drink order if you want to get it!"

It's catch up time. Lance is hesitant and just looks at Jenn. She's annoyed. Pissed off at him. *Really? You do this every fucking time.*

"I'll take them. Help me get the drinks from the bar and I'll take over everything."

Jenn demands that Isabel get her shit together. She's a leader by heart but doesn't quite know how to fully take control of that part of her personality.

"Who's the manager?" drools out Lance.

"It's Dante for the closer." Isabel says as she's walking them over to the POS to get them clocked in. Lance is slow to accept that this is how his night is going to be. He's in denial and doesn't want to work a busy shift and doesn't want to accept that he may actually have to lift up one of his thick fingers to get something done. He's at work; he has to be there for at least six hours, and *still,* he can't be bothered to do his fucking job while he's standing there. This is something that's incredibly disappointing to Jenn. Jenn has quit several things, but she tries until she can't try, or until she's put down by an opposing influence. Who's going to stop to tell her she's not good enough to be a waitress?

That party of four is a bitch. Her first table, her first greet of the day, and she's treated like shit. Constantly yelling about how poor the service is and how there are no refills on their drinks. She doesn't even know what they're drinking because she just walked in but she can see clearly that these are the kind of people who will complain that they have too many or too few ice cubes in her drink. She goes into the back of house and finds a mess. Voices come from all around her, screaming demands. She can't pinpoint who they are coming from, or why they are even being shouted. She's flustered but keeps her emotions intact. She shows no fear, and no remorse. This is something she can do.

She brings back the refills, greets her other three tables that are not even in the same area taking care of others along the way. Other servers are scratching to get out while they still can and won't go near the dining room until they have paid in and clocked out. She picks up a local draft beer from the bar and as she is off to deliver it, a patron roars at her.

"SCUSE ME MISS!"

She freezes in stride.

"I haven't got to my server in 10 minutes. Can you bring me some extra ranch and we need more drinks. Please!"

Now she stuck completing the tasks of others. She delivers the beer, then goes to the line to pick up some ranch. It's empty. There's not enough to even fake the idea that she made an effort. She looks to fill the dressing up since that's what she does, the things that others won't. She goes to the walk-in freezer where all the dressings are kept. She looks for the ranch and sees him. Out of the corner of her eyes she spots him, bent over, holding his own sides. She can't believe it. Lance is almost unrecognizable. He has this dark desperation in his eyes as they swell up; he's cold and just sitting there. Jenn was too busy to notice that he disappeared. She asks him the simple question. "Are you okay?"

That's all it takes. Asked easily to make small talk with anyone, the one question that's asked 1,000 times every day to every customer in the world, and a question that requires almost no thought to answer. Lance had to think about it long and hard. Has she ever asked him this question? He breaks down and tears fall down his face. He hit the wall. He doesn't want to be here anymore but he can't find a way to express it. The only thing that Jenn can respond with is a simple answer.

"It's okay. It's gonna be okay. We can talk at home. Are you going to make it?"

He doesn't know. He just cries.

"I'll be back." she responded to him. She still has a job to do and she's going to see it through this time. Until this moment Jenn's never seen this man shed a single tear for anything. Like all of his pain just shot out like a bullet. She almost felt bad for him.

After she completes her tasks at hand and gets her tables in order she looks for him in the cooler only to find that he's not there. She asks around and everyone says he never came to work. *How's that fucking possible,* she thinks. They drove in together, so how did he get to leave? At the same time, she doesn't really care anymore. She's through with it. All she can feel now is pity. So when Lance finally walks up to her she's made up her mind.

"Where did you go? I was lookin' for you."

"I was in the restroom."

"What happened?"

"I...just...didn't feel..."

Jenn is noticing this hesitation in his words. Lance is a man that has never once said anything meaningful or serious to her. Seeing his eyes red and swollen pushes Jenn to realize that she doesn't want him. She doesn't want to settle anymore. She wants to be her own woman. She wants to pursue what she wants, drink what she wants, work where she wants, fuck who she wants.

"When you get home tonight, I think you should leave."

Lance doesn't say anything. It's almost like this is what he wanted but didn't have the balls to do it himself. He tries throughout their busy shift to say something and get through to her but she's too busy to take the time and doesn't want to waste any time on him. He doesn't believe she is done with him. Lance continues to greet and feed his tables while questioning what all is going on between him and Jenn. All he wants to do is explain the emotional stress and confusion he's hid from his girlfriend and peers. He feels like an ass and wants to get closure from Jenn. Closure doesn't exist in the restaurant industry. Like wondering how a server can receive a shitty tip from a friendly customer. It happens, and there's no logical explanation as to why. Lance finally gives up looking for Jenn and decides to take his break in the restroom, only to find Dante fucking her in the bathroom stall. Dante doesn't notice his presence but Jenn moans and looks directly at him and winks. Three minutes later, they both walked to the front together. Lance doesn't say anything to Jenn for the entire shift and packs all of his things when they get home.

X. Dante's Inferno

It's a busy day at the casual eatery but people are mostly pleasant. It's wild, and hungry people are lining up waiting to be sat and fed. Amidst the tension of empty stomachs and, of course, another shift that would benefit by having a few more servers, Dante is laughing uncontrollably. Some of the more irate customers are looking at him with confusion. What bitter fools they are.

As Dante collects himself wiping the tears from his face, he runs to Jordan pointing at him.

"This guy. This fuckin' guy right here!"

"What?"

"Your table came up to me." He can barely enunciate his words as his chuckling makes him almost incomprehensible.

"Your table told me how rude you were. Quit being an asshole to your tables man!"

He just laughs harder. It's a hard laugh with its own pulse at 100 bpm piercing Jordan's ears. He shutters at every sound and grows annoyed with each gesture.

"I didn't do anything to them!"

"Yeah, you didn't! That's the fuckin' problem man! They said, listenlisten, they said it's horrible. Couldn't believe that we hire people like you. I ask, well, what do you mean? They said, get this, getthisgetthis...they said it's shameful and against God to be hirin' people like you!"

"What did you do to them?" Jordan's becoming tired of Dante's antics. He knows that he's fucking with him, and he wants to walk away, but, he wants to hear this story and see how it plays out. Something about him that keeps other servers and workers around and gravitating towards him.

"I'm like... hey, that's just fucking Jordan man, once you know him he's a nice guy! I don't think they want to get to know you. Fuckin' old people..."

Jordan didn't find anything he said to be funny, but Dante's still giggling to himself.

"Come man, you know that shit's funny. That table was a trip!"

He observes the restaurant from his imaginary throne. Dante runs the place and is fully aware of how to work the system against itself. Something he takes pride in.

"I need something to drink. It's this schwag that Vince sold me."

"You should know better than to get weed from him."

"It was free! No wonder. I need to get out of here so I can get my real shit."

Dante usually works under some type of substance but because of low potent weed that Vicente is selling, he's doing the shift sober. Normally, he carries some blow with him but he's saving it for a better time. He just wants to get high or feel some type of buzz, and he'll go far and beyond to get it. Any moment of sobriety to him is completely out of his thought. He's afraid that if he stops, he'll wake up to a hangover from 15 years of hard drug and alcohol abuse. He thinks in order to get through this shift he'll need to be in a different dimension. Some other level of existence that his lowly humble co-workers know nothing about. His job is second nature to him and he's scheming in his head where to get his next score. Until then, he's going to settle for something that he has easy access to: alcohol. Dante knows where to go to get it. He's been getting away with it for four years. His methods are becoming

sloppy and he is beginning to leave a trail. Perhaps
Charlie and Alden are becoming privy to the situation,
but either way, at this point, Dante is no more interested
in his job than he is his addictions.

Dante is about to share his feelings about the universe
with Jordan but just as he does, Lance walks up to him
like a zombie.

"Hey, I need your help."

"Fuck man, I'm talkin here."

"I forgot to ring up Table 33. I need their shi—stuff,
on the fly."

"What? WHAT! You're joking! You're fucking with
me! You're JOKING! I can't believe my ears!"

"Yeah, I thought I put it in..."

"Christ almighty. Come with me."

He walks to the back of house. The line is dirty, and
filled with dinner plates. Sauces are all over and the
cooks are beginning to fall behind.

"Oh, what the *fuck* is going on back here?! This food
is fucking dying! Get this shit out of here!"

Dante screams at everyone. His yelling is so loud that
his voice can be heard at the entrance of the restaurant.
His presence intimidates some of the smaller servers like
Isabel, and some of the self-conscious servers like Lance.

"Everyone STOP! WHAT THE FUCK IS GOING
ON BACK HERE! HEY ... REAL QUICK—ADOLFO

...33... I NEED THAT SHIT ON THE FLY ... FUCK-UP OVER HERE CAN'T SEEM TO GET HIS HAND OFF HIS DICK!"

Dante takes control. His wrath freezes the staff and he demands their work to come.

"HEY! ALL OF YOU, STOP WHAT THE FUCK YOU'RE DOING AND RUN THIS FUCKING FOOD. ISABEL, PUT DOWN THE ICE SCOOP AND GET YOUR FUCKIN' ASS OVER HERE. GODDAMN IT! GET THIS SHIT OUT IT'S DYING. RE-COOKS ARE COMING OUT OF YOUR FUCKIN' TIPS!"

Dante seems to be getting the kitchen together but is still pissed off because his quality boy Vicente is missing. He looks at Lance.

"WELL? What the fuck are you still doing here? Run this shit! WHERE THE FUCK IS VINCE PENDEJOS? I bet I know where that fucker is. Taking a shit. HEY FUCK HEADS, IF YOU HAVE TO TAKE A SHIT, PLEASE FOR THE LOVE OF ALL THAT IS CHANDLER'S TELL SOMEONE TO WATCH YOUR GODDAMN STATION."

Vicente flushes the toilet in the employee restroom and slowly walks out.

"Hey! Vince, good going dipshit. Tell me when you're leaving, and get some better weed. Get your shit caught up."

Dante cleans himself in the sink next to the line where the food comes out and then Lance comes back up.

"How's the food going?"

"What? It's coming out. You have to wait for it to get cooked. Food can't come out raw you stupid bitch!"

Dante doesn't show any remorse for his words or for what he does. He doesn't care for these workers. The thoughts of his staff, just like the thought of his actions, don't follow him to the next step he takes.

"Hey before you go crying off, what the hell did you do to Jenn to make her into a whore?"

Lance doesn't say anything. His feelings are obviously hurt but he's trying his hardest to hide them. Lance will not be there when the shift is over.

"Dante!" shouts Isabel.

"Yes."

"I need a rewards discount on Table 16."

"Fuck, am I the only one here? Where the hell is jumbo-face?"

"Charlie? He left 30 minutes ago."

"Come here."

Dante leads her to the nearest computer. He types in his numbers and pulls up the table. In a single motion, he applies a discount code that gives the customer 40% off. Dante's prowess over the computer system and the world of the industry is rivaled only by the GM, Alden. He's efficient, smart, and a horrible human being.

After this task, Dante goes directly to the liquor. He brings two to-go cups that most of the staff drink out of through the shift and pours himself a beer in one and bourbon in the other. He walks straight back to the office and hides it with a lid and straw. He gulps down what he can of the bourbon and just waits.

Dante's shift always rewards itself with great prizes. Alcohol, women, drugs, all of it. Once he feels the beginning of his new alcohol buzz, he is now ready to go out and talk to tables. All of a sudden the man who was yelling out profanities greets each table with grace and elegance. He says various one-liners but usually sticks with the basics:

"Hello! How are you! How was your meal? What brought you out? Are you coming back? I hope to see you! Ask for Jenn! Jordan is the best man we have!"

He's a good-looking man, tall, not fit but not fat. He smells but his stench blends in with the surroundings. No customer notices because they aren't close enough. He often smells like smoke and other restaurant scents. His

149

beard is trimmed and his hair is styled—meticulously messy, with every hair in its place. The servers don't care how anyone looks, smells, or feels. Nobody working in the trenches of the overfed really cares that his shoes were covered in kitchen shit, raw meat, and bleach. Everyone shares the same floor with each other. After each round of talking to tables he'll walk to Jordan to give his perception of reality.

"Who are *these fucks* to judge when everyone here all shares the same sin? Every day it's something. It's not just a few people; it's everyone. The customers, the mothers, the business owners. Everyone has a dark secret to tell and when they eat at our restaurant, that's when it comes out. Right? It seems that we are but a hub for secrets. Like a cheap therapy. The stories we hear all of the time. The laziness in people. The selfishness. Judgmental whores."

The alcohol is kicking in. Dante gets philosophical when the buzz takes control of his mind. Pretty soon, his words will sound like gibberish to everyone but him, but his confidence sells that gibberish to sound like something meaningful.

Jordan just stares blankly at him. How does Dante fucking do it? Talk so much shit without a care in the world. *What happened to this man for him to be this way?* Jordan is out of the conversation and paying no attention to Dante's monologue. His mouth is just moving. The sounds from the restaurant drown out his words. He chimes back in and hears him on a completely different subject. Jordan wonders how long he's been here. What seems like hours is actually only a few minutes. Jordan is thinking about one thing. He's thinking about *her*. He always thinks about his love. It's his obsession. Just as he snaps out of it, Dante somehow starts talking about women and girls again. Dante's other addiction. Jordan wonders if he said something to get him on this subject.

"Ugly girls are the best. Their self-esteem is low, so it's easy to make them feel good with just a smile. They will give it all. Especially after they're dumped. Let me tell you why Lance is walking out of here tonight..."

Jordan senses something different in Dante's tone. It seems far more sinister than when he started. There's nothing pure about what he says anymore. It all seems like a game. Lance is broken, John left, and now Jordan finds himself questioning things he was so sure of one week ago.

Dante and Jordan worked at Chandler's long enough to see almost everything that could happen at a restaurant. They did the minimum, had their fun, and fucked around but subtly something inside Jordan began to grow in a space that Dante didn't have. Dante continues to speak without clarification or context as he often does. The moments and opportunities for pleasure dictates his nature.

"These women aren't beautiful at all. They are ugly on the inside. That's why they put so much fucking time in their looks. Look at that bitch at 34. What's she hiding? They literally fuckin' mask themselves with makeup, brands, and other shit. It's horrible that societal implications have such a major impact on these poor girls. Yet at the same time, it makes it easier to fuck with them. I bet I can get a date with her."

He pauses.

"You know what? Close up shop and get the hell out of here."

Dante leaves Jordan behind, confused and then creeps along the side of the wall and dances up to Hannah. Hannah just laughs it off and isn't aware of how much alcohol or buzz he is feeling. He sees something inside her. He wants to see inside her.

"I want you and Andrea to close up shop tonight."

Dante pulls out his phone and then sends a text to his wife.

WILL BE LATE GOTTA CLOSE UP WITH SOME NEWBIES.

Chandler's is Dante's playground.

XI. Employee Discount

It's Monday night. Hannah the Hostess works slowly and without any pressure. Last Monday was a lot busier, but tonight, only a few tables every 20 minutes or so and because of this, servers were sent home towards the beginning of their shift without any money to take home. Dante decided to keep Hannah on until closing time. She is too young, so she knows everything. The whole world is in front of her for the taking and she can do as she pleases though she's not a troublemaker; she just fools herself into thinking she is. The simple-minded young girl who is "mature" enough to make the right choices in life is a junior in high school. She won't date anyone her age. She thinks she enjoys older men; not like the kids that may be in college, but the other type— her teachers, her managers, her father's co-workers. Naivety and its pure innocence creates her world. This is the attention she craves, but has never received. She would be happy for a hug but really she just wants to be wanted and cared for. Unfortunately, she is unaware that she really *doesn't* know the difference between good and bad attention, but she'll soon come to find that she never wanted any of it at all.

All of the men that work here at Chandler's are scummy enough to take advantage of such young prime meat. They'll try to sway her, wow her, and win her affection but Hannah doesn't play into their games, primarily because she doesn't know what those games are. She's been hit on several times but doesn't take the cue unless the wonderfully romantic men ask her straight for a naked picture of her or to do this or that. It's unabated blissfulness. She's only heard stories about sex and never thought that she would be a girl who would be teased for not drinking, smoking, or giving head. Yet, the girls who work with her converse about it constantly and look at Hannah like she is the freak simply because she doesn't give into pressure.

Despite her overly inviting looks, the care taken to ensure her pouty lips are always glossed and her outfits are always current and suggestive. The saying "take a picture—it'll last longer" couldn't be more applicable to Hannah's existence, as she warrants stares and gaping jaws from boys, men, and even girls. She is half Hispanic, half Caucasian, with a mother that's barely double her age. Her chest sticks out beautifully and perky like one of a well endowed pop singer, or even porn star, which she covers up under a simple buttoned down black shirt that puckers ever so slightly at the third button. She is taller than most girls hovering around 5'9" with legs long and always shaved even under long pants in a cold winter. She has light brown eyes, almost doe-like, warm and inviting to the many customers that walk through the doors. Her hair waves are like where the ocean meets the coast, perfectly shaped, equidistant from each strand. She has a small beauty mark on the left side of her face, right beneath her eye. When she smiles, her face seems engulfed by her sparkling teeth framed perfectly by her lips.

It's five minutes until closing time. Hannah is waiting to be cut by Dante and she's waiting for her ride to come pick her up. At least that's what her story is to everyone else. The closing hostess is sitting there at the stand waiting for something to happen; whether it's the cute busser with long eyelashes and dark hair, a table to walk in, or servers to bitch about why they are still here.

The only reason this place gets business is because of the area it is centralized in. On Monday nights, the restaurant is usually a place where the middle-aged blue collar people come in and have their night out. Most of these people work at the distribution center down the highway and often have Tuesday and Wednesday as their days off and work through the weekend.

Hannah always works Monday night because of seniority. Normally she doesn't close, but tonight a hostess wanted to leave early so she could sneak off when her parents were asleep. Hannah and Andrea, the other hostess, get along just fine; it's the other girls that they don't like. Most of the very young workers get their job through connections. It's very rare that you see a straggler come in, and it is even rarer that you see them get along with everyone here.

Hannah smiles and imagines herself to be in Andrea's situation. Having a boyfriend coming in to get her. Taking her to a nice place on top of a hill where they can stare at all the city lights and talk and hold one another. She has hope to be a romantic. Before the kitchen closes she walks back to the office and asks Dante if she can order food. He tells her she can have whatever she wants, as long as it's not a ribeye or a lobster. Hannah knows what she's going to order. She's been craving it all day long really, and in her mind, why would she get anything else?

People in the back of the restaurant are still cleaning up the mess that everyone else caused and are so focused on getting off. Hannah skips to a server that's still working the dining room to take care of her order.

"I'll take the chicken tenders with buffalo sauce, some fries, and an extra side of ranch. Don't forget the extra side!"

"Did you want something to drink?"

The corner of her perfect lips curls up deviously. "Soda."

"What kind? Do you want soda, or *soda?* Wink wink, nudge nudge."

"Can you get *soda?* Will Dante notice?"

The server chuckles and huffs to himself. "Be back in a sec."

She begins to wait for her food and she gets her soda, which the manager nefariously poured himself. This is a special soda. The kind that only the manager can make, and that only she can ask for, the kind with the lovely kick of spiced rum. She accepts his offer and gladly sucks on the straw with the utmost pleasure. The tingling sensation consumes her as she swallows every bit of rum inside that soft drink. Hannah then asks for another, something a bit *stronger.* Something with more *flavor* added. Dante delivers this one personally. After she suckles down her drink to almost nothing, she begins to get a very big craving for something to eat.

The tenders get lightly battered to give this perfect crisp in every bite. Then, once the chicken is fried to golden, crunchy brown, it's removed, drained of excess oil, and sauce is poured all over. The cook on duty tosses to coat every single tender with this milder version of a buffalo sauce. While the sauce isn't too spicy, it is hot enough to set Hannah's delicate mouth on fire. Fries are thrown without care on the side of the plate but stacked extremely high. The fries are a bit thinner than usual, but nevertheless are salted with perfection and, when dipped in the right flavor and sauce, taste extraordinary. Just perfect for Hannah's cravings. Once plated by restaurant standards, it is taken with care and put near a huge bowl of ranch. Hannah receives her plate and smiles with ecstasy. She grabs her fork and cuts a perfect bite-sized piece of chicken and then dips it into the bowl of creamy ranch. The food is so hot that it burns her tongue, and she lets out a small hissing sound from her throat. The ranch drips from the bite-sized piece onto her plate, creating drops of this mixture of buffalo and ranch. That is something that Hannah loves, as she grabs her fries and dips it in her newly mixed sauce. She eats every bite off her plate, slowly as if she's finely dining in a restaurant. She feels the grandeur as she fantasizes what life will be like when she's just a little bit older.

Finally she finishes and exhales in bliss and pleasure. She couldn't have another bite, but then, Dante brings her dessert. Dante mumbles something to himself about her body as he approaches her. Quiet enough for only him to hear but loud enough for Hannah to register the vibrations in the air.

"What?" she asks.

"I want you to know that you can stay as long as you need. Do you need another drink?"

"Yeah!" she screams with excitement.

"You know you're one the best workers here." He leans in closer to her and gets on one knee so she can see him on eye level.

"No I'm not." She says laughing. The liquor is beginning to show itself through those big brown eyes. She's becoming loose and carefree not yet realizing that this isn't the buzz adults get when they drink.

"Yeah. You really are." Dante continues. "You don't complain. Ever. Everyone else does. You come in and you're always so happy. Always so perky."

"I don't need...I'm not going to be able—" She stops. She wasn't aware liquor had this type of impact on her body.

"Please." He says so calmly. "Don't worry. I want to show my gratitude."

Dessert comes right before she can take the moment in. Dante is in the back making sure she gets fed just right and that nobody does her wrong—you can't do something wrong to something so beautiful. That would be a sin. Hannah gets her chocolate layered brownie placed right in front of her. She doesn't want it, but she doesn't say no. She didn't ask for it, but here it is. In front of her. Waiting for her to taste. This time, she takes it slow. She savors every bit, every flavor, every swallow. She learned from dinner that slow is the best way to go.

Dante walks out and gets back down on his knees resting his arm behind her without Hannah realizing.

"It's good, right? I made it."

She eats it so slow that closing time comes and goes. The waiting staff goes away and off into their own plans. Hannah is still there, alone, eating and drinking all that she can. She feels good, too good to know how or why she even feels this way. She is jovial and jumping on the inside, while trying to put all her energies in not collapsing from her gluttonous state. Dante comes by and checks on her every couple of minutes or so as he is signing the closers out in between visits.

"How is it?" Dante is very interested in his best worker. "What are your plans after school? Need another drink? You're the best I've ever had."

All of a sudden Hannah is lost. She closes her eyes and opens them slowly. She's dizzy. She's turning her head and sees the tables twist around in a quick frenzy.

"I should go. I'm not feeling so good." She is in a trance, feeling bad about her state of mind, but at the same time completely relaxed. Almost too relaxed.

"No, it's okay." Dante's voice changes. He only speaks in this tone to his wife...and his girlfriend, and his other boyfriend.

"What do you mean? I feel weird."

"That's normal. It's fun right?"

"I don't know."

"Here, let me put on some music and we can dance. Everyone dances. Do you dance?"

"Well. I'm a dancer at school."

"No kidding?"

"Yeah."

"I bet you're the best dancer in the whole school."

"I'm okay"

"Show me."

"Here? Show you?"

"Yeah? Show me. Don't be shy show me. What do you like to dance to?"

"I mean, I couldance to anythin' really." Hannah is unaware that her words are beginning to slur.

"Yeah? I like dance music. Like the EDM stuff. Even the old Kylie Minogue. That was probably when you were very little."

"Yeah... if I ca'dance to it, I likeit." She scoffs and smirks to herself staring blankly at Dante. Her slurring becomes more apparent.

"Here's an old one called 'Satisfaction.' It's by a guy called Benassi."

He plugged his phone into the stereo system.

Frost is starting to form on the grass from another cold front. From a far distance any person could see inside as the interior is still very well lit. Dante is watching. Sitting in silence amused by her fluctuation and he inches towards her.

* * *

Hannah wakes puffing, panting and brawling with her own breath. She can't seem to catch a normal rhythm and she's completely unaware of her surroundings. Her heart is racing and her head is pulsating through her eyes. It's still dark out and she doesn't realize she's in the back of a car that doesn't belong to her. The frost is surrounding the windows but she recognizes the neon light outline through the ice. She's still in the Chandler's parking lot.

She's dressed, but her hair is messy and curled up from being wet, but from what she wonders. Her clothes are barely hanging on and she is not wearing the coat she came to work with. She looks for her phone in a panic. She wonders how she got here and what caused her to black out. She wasn't drinking that much, or so she thought. She honestly didn't know how much was too much. It's hard to tell when she's never had a drink before now. She tried to move her leg to sit up but she's stiff. It's cold enough in the car that she can see her breath even though she's not outside. Her leg is stuck and it feels bruised.

Before she finishes the thought in her mind about what happened, she reaches around to her back and notices that, one, she's not wearing her underwear anymore, and two, there is something sticky that is keeping her shirt on her skin. Her hands begin to shake violently.

One moment she was enjoying her free dinner, and now she's cold and alone in the dark, like an empty beer can. She doesn't remember saying no to him but she doesn't remember saying yes.

She tries to open the door, but it's locked. She climbs to the front door and lets herself out and immediately falls to the ground. Hannah looks around, shivers and folds her arms across her chest. She has no balance and nobody can see her as she walks away from the car and searches for her own. She stumbles across the parking lot attempting to walk 10 yards to her new Ford her father purchased for her. The delightful feeling from earlier is transformed into a new reality. With each step she feels a whirling sensation that starts from her ankle as it struggles to keep her balanced and shoots straight to her head in a forceful pain. If this is what happens when people drink, she doesn't ever want to own this sensation again. Her eyes open in shock. She can't find her keys. She wonders if she left them inside. She turns around and there he is.

"Hannah!" Dante yells from the back employee entrance of the restaurant. "You're the best employee I've ever had. Be careful going home. I'll see you tomorrow."

He smiles at her. Dante throws the keys towards her. They land on the ground a few inches away from where she is standing and slides under the car. Hannah begins rubbing her eyes as if she's looking at a mirage, unable to identify what is happening.

"Watch what you drink. You passed out on me. Be careful."

She is powerless against his force and is bombarded with emotional questions and guilt that rattle her brain. She begins to blame herself for it all. Dante walks off into the night with his hands in his coat. Hannah gets on her knees and looks for her keys. She opens her door, heats it up, and tries to keep the windshield from turning. She can barely move, let alone drive.

In the morning she knows it'll be different. She will be shattered.

XII. Stiffed

The Beginning

Life revolved around the tips that the servers make. Good tips, bad tips; they all went to the same thing. Every cent worked for, and cried for, the staff spent on each other. The industry created a very specific, almost cult-like lifestyle to mold the staff by using drugs, alcohol, and sex. That's how the employees work in the front of house. That's how Jordan knew it when he began. That's how he worked, lived, and slept. After any shift, morning, or night, they'd go out with their earnings instead of going home. They felt like they were the richest fuckers in the world and Jordan would always spend like there was no tomorrow because oftentimes the collective anxiety of all the servers would lead him to believe that there wasn't a tomorrow. Their philosophical outlook on life revolved around living in the moment, but the moment never lasted very long. He thought he was hot shit and invincible and loved it when his coworkers would come over, cook out, and just drink, smoke and do anything they wanted. The people in his circle didn't have kids, and didn't have credit, just the moments with one another. Moments making money while doing the minimum. As Jordan survived the staff where others hadn't, he began to notice certain trends that would cause all the servers to not have to think for themselves.

The workers at Chandler's would share way more than a normal group should share: food, drinks, cigarettes, receipes, rides, music, movies, secrets, men, women, money, sex, beds, homes, and their souls. There was nothing to be ashamed of. Collectively, they also shared the notion that it's not right to be ashamed to want something specific. The customers do it all of the time. Jordan sees them multiple times a day. Without shame, the patrons of Chandler's cry, scream, and pout for what they want and don't stop until it's delivered.

So, like the guests, Jordan and the staff often are unashamed when it came to sex and fulfilling their own desires. To the workers of Chandler's, sex wasn't a favor, it was returning a favor. A way of saying thanks without having to awkwardly say thanks. There's not a better thank you than oral sex.

That was the best thing about the end of the day and having the opportunity to *know* the staff. They may not be friends for life, but the friends and relationships come with the job and once Jordan leaves the job, he was fully aware that his presence will fade too. He hopes to leave a memory and lasting impression on someone.

166

New challenges arose for every person with problems only unique to their personality. Jordan's unique personality problem was, and has always been, Meredith.

It seemed everyone had a vice and it was easy to find out what it was. The "regular" people that were outside of Jordan's group had them too, albeit they were not as destructive. Jordan knew he wasn't "normal" and knew that something was different. Something made him *special.*

However, nobody is unique; everyone is made of the same emotions. Normal is a point of view shared only by the individual. What Jordan, Dante, and their friends considered to be normal were those who went home to their families. Those who worked for something else in the future. The temporaries and outsiders...the weirdos...the ones who came to work for only the work. Jordan, along with Meredith, John, Lance, Jenn, Isabel, and others didn't understand them. They didn't have a clue what they were doing. They were lost with ambitions but nowhere to take them.

It was a shared unspoken experience that didn't necessarily lead them to hurt, or internal pain. The fear of failure kept them from going anywhere, or maybe they are living the life that they perceive to deserve. Either way, they could do it all by having a little fun and experiencing something only a small percentage of people get to experience.

Whenever Jordan has a gathering at his house, sex was on everyone's mind. Dante would feed into this idea that sex is an ice breaker. The two men would often play a game of guessing who would go home with who and how. The gatherings always started with drugs but their inhibitions were lost through shots and sometimes needles.

When it was time to let loose, Jordan didn't hesitate to tell Meredith how he really felt and why. When it came down to it, Meredith enjoyed his attention and was always fascinated that he felt so strongly about her sloppy self. They weren't the hottest people, but at a certain point in life and at a certain job, the only requirement to score is to be human and not ugly. No matter if a person was big, small, fat, skinny, a saint, or a devil, it was like a meal when feeling hungry. This staff was fucking starving and Jordan and Meredith's appetite couldn't be met with just a simple kiss. After they fucked a few times in the dark, Meredith would always tell him in her rants that kisses didn't hold any meaning of affection, or any of the conceptual thoughts at all. The only time kisses meant something was when they were naked inside each other.

The Choice

Time can't keep Jordan from making the wrong choice over and over. After the first time Meredith took Jordan to bed, they were locked in forever. Trapped by a force that was unknown. No matter what they did, who else they saw, every day their minds would be on each other in a deep passionate infatuation. Maybe love? They weren't sure what it was, but Meredith knew she couldn't be in love with Jordan. She was engaged; she couldn't possibly love him. Jordan isn't a man that she would want to marry, and she definitely could not see herself with this loser of a man in the future. She couldn't build a life with him because he didn't have the job that her fiancé had. Jordan was confused, and her future husband wasn't.

Yet, Meredith always wanted his attention, and romanticized everything about him. His confused personality of trying to find himself reassured Meredith that it was okay to feel like shit and actually show it. To Meredith, Jordan wasn't there unless she wanted her to be. He was used, and didn't seem to mind it. He liked her calls and was always waiting for them, despite her wedding date coming closer and closer. Jordan knew this and he was using her, too. He was using her to create a new sense of purpose for himself; he was using her for that release of oxytocin and endorphins. He chased that, he needed that escape, and it felt good to get it whenever he could, especially if it came in different doses, and in different substances other than alcohol and drugs. Sex was just as addicting, if not more, and sex with Meredith was the perfect way to unwind after getting shamed and yelled at. They were never really any good for each other but it didn't matter. Meredith could do things with Jordan that she could not do with her man. They never took their relationship to work, but everyone still knew.

Jordan couldn't really find the words to describe the feelings he felt but continued to walk in with no reason, answer Meredith's call and give her what she needed when she needed it. Meredith was completely depressed in her relationship but never admitted it to anyone. Admitting that takes courage and Meredith didn't have any. She avoided the issue by letting Jordan have his way with her instead of talking about it with the "love of her life." In one instance, she had the girl-balls to call Jordan up while her future husband was lying right next to her, and invited him to come out to the Graveyard. Instead of waking her fiancé up and talking about what's bothering her, she came to the conclusion that going out with another man and venting about it would be better.

"He doesn't do...so many things that you do. I don't think he understands me like the way you do, but I'm so confused."

"We understand each other, we always have."

What a load of cat shit. How would this man know he didn't respect or understand Meredith if Meredith was silent about it? He can't read minds and her fiancé was shitty at reading body language and facial cues.

Her fiancé worked all the time and when Jordan and Meredith were off, she would invite Jordan to go out on dates to eat, have coffee, go bowling, and even watch a movie. Jordan just wanted to stay home and drink and fuck because he knew that they weren't together in a traditional sense. Jordan began to fall for her in these tiny moments. He began to understand her mannerisms unlike anyone else and knew what to do to make her smile. His addiction. His dependency.

Why can't she just leave him and be with me? Why am I even going along with this?

Is she embarrassed by me? Am I what she wants? If not then why the fuck is she doing this?

He questioned this more and more every time he came on her lower back. He wasn't like Dante; he couldn't sever that connection so easily. Maybe she didn't feel the way he did.

It never really occurred to Jordan how much trouble one person could cause. It never did when he said hello and invited her over to his house to have a beer after work. When she was the only one to show up. Alone. Before he knew she was taken.

Meredith never said her true intentions or hinted that she wanted to stop. Her wedding was weeks away and she stayed there. Always there. Always hurting. But with her being with *him,* Jordan needed to find out if he could reach out once more to find some type of happiness. He'll never find it because really, it never existed. *Jordan* barely existed. After one night in bed, she got up and looked at him. She said she couldn't do this anymore. That it was over. She's getting married. Isn't that a fun thing to hear after she coerced him into *her* bedroom. She tells him this while he is lying where her future husband will be.

The Wedding

That was another moment of humiliation. Heart-crushing, fist-to-your-fucking-face humiliation. That is, except for shy glances, whispered secrets, and butterflies. Except for ...certain things. All Jordan could do was look back hoping that she'll remember why they were together doing their cheating thing to begin with.

Their wedding was shit. Jordan was invited and came with Dante. It was in a small hall behind a smaller church. Barely 25 people were there. It seemed that

Meredith was actually going through with it. When Jordan went to the small room in the back to give the bride best wishes in private, she was already drunk. He couldn't believe it but then he had hope. After the bride and groom said their vows, the bride disappeared. She passed out in the room where she waited to be taken down the aisle. Jordan knew then that it wouldn't last. Jordan cursed the world to Dante and spilled his guts out, and then all of a sudden, her wonderful man, who she chose over the complex Jordan, pissed himself and threw a punch at his brother and started a brawl. Dante and Jordan watched as this redneck wreck took place.

"Want to go to a bar?" asked Dante.

"No. Let's see how this plays out."

The Unnecessary Ending

Today Jordan wakes up and thinks about this woman, who isn't beautiful, but still holds a chain around his dick. Meredith.

A young woman, beyond her years with strong curves and bags under her eyes. Eyes that Jordan could never get right. They were green some days, and other days they were blue. She wears glasses on busy days in the restaurants and Jordan only recognizes her when they finish those long shifts. Jordan never knew a woman like her existed. So caring towards her workers, and empathetic towards her customers, even though the customers are fools.

The relationship turns darker with every passing day. The marriage didn't stop her from searching for the missing hole in her heart. The only thing she can fill the void with is Jordan's poisonous affection. They are no longer just having sex, but now taking their frustrations on each other and their meet ups became more frequent. Bitter, pissed off, aggressive and almost abusive and destructive sex. They are now accustomed to liking it rough. Hair pulling, spanking, hitting, throwing, and choking are becoming more and more commonplace. Their sex is filled with rage as if they are screaming. *Why?*

The questions about their relationship can only be expressed through sexual play. They piss each other off but have no other outlet to express their pain because their secret runs so deep.

Why did you marry him? To which Meredith will reply by digging her nails in his back wondering *why the fuck did you let me get married and why didn't you stop me?* As they orgasm they'll both scream at each other with full intentions asking *why are we doing this to each other?*

They'll argue that this will be the last time they'll ever talk but...

She calls him aside during the shift, and tells him like a friend that she'll be seeing him tonight. Nobody objects and it is now normal. Meredith's husband knows what she's doing because her love towards him seems unsensual, unappealing, and even disgusting. Boring. Bland. Like oatmeal in the morning, but without the sugar, cinnamon, or fruits. Just oats and water. It's not like that with Jordan.

She grabs her food before she gets ready to leave and finishes her work. Meredith walks to the corner of the restaurant. Table 21. It's clean and she calls Jordan to meet her through text and thinks it's better she does it now than to do it in the middle of the night after they fuck each other up and over, figuratively and literally. Jordan approaches her.

"I can't see you after all tonight."

"Why not?"

"He's checking everything I do. He's questioning me all the time. I'm sure he knows. He for sure knows that we aren't going to make it."

"Are you going to stay with him?"

"Yes, I have to."

"Why?"

"I don't have to explain myself to you. You're not my fuckin' husband."

"Fuck you! You don't actually...but after..."

"What?"

Jordan wants to yell at her. He doesn't know how. He doesn't know how to take out his pain in any other form than drinking and sex. He's lost and can't come up with the words. He feels something very strong inside him but cannot place the emotion to a thought or the thought to the emotion. He's hurt and hurting bad. He's feeling like a complete dick. He's getting broken up with a woman who's not even with him at a table where he received a 35% tip, his highest in a long while. He can't explain that both of them made the same mistake over and over and that he actually loves her and cares for her and wants her in the banal way of wanting a person.

It's good that one of them chose to end it. No longer are they capable of continuing to act like everything is fine while on the inside both of them scream, cry, and hurt themselves with hypotheticals. Both were born crying in the night and now they can't even have the capacity to shed a tear for one another. Both are numb. It seems like they had to constantly search for each other inside their rooms. The only place where they could be truly who they are. Screaming in agony while the other is screaming in pleasure.

Meredith walks off. Jordan gets his things and goes home. On his drive he thinks maybe he'll go to church in the morning and think of something or someone better to do with his free time. *Nobody has any hope for me so why should God think anything different?* Jordan lowers his standards, confidence, and everything else. Today and every day he feels he should be a voice of optimism, but he doesn't know how. He feels like he should call her, stop her, say something to her but he doesn't know how to begin or even where to begin. He tells himself over and over that everything will be okay even though he knows that tomorrow will be horrible. The night will be horrible and he just needs to move on. The closest he will get will be seeing her in passing at the restaurant. He should've woken up from the nightmare long ago but he didn't and enjoyed the dream while it lasted. Until then, he'll go spend his time in the Graveyard.

Maybe salvation won't be there for him, but he won't know if he doesn't leave it alone. His false messiah came to him cloaked in sensuality, striking with an open hand and inviting him to do the same. Her toxic words dripped from her lips—the same ones he worshipped and sacrificed himself to taste. When he is out in his nightly ritual at the Graveyard, suddenly he receives a text from Meredith. Why hasn't he blocked the number? She tells him to come get her. The text is urgent in all caps pleading with him.

PLEASE PLEASE PLEASE

He looks to pay the tab and as he is trying to call her she is already doing the same thing. He picks up the phone and instead of the playful voice he is accustomed to hearing he hears tears, sniffles, and rambling. He can barely make out what she's saying. It's so hard to tell under her tears. She wants him to come over? Something must be wrong. The only thing he understands is her saying to come over now. He hangs up then gets the text.

HOW FAR ARE YOU AWAY? WHEN WILL YOU BE HERE?

He flies away to get her. He flies, like he loves, like a part of him is falling down from the night with a great beam dust trail shimmering behind him. He doesn't normally feel like this when he sees her but when he arrives, the door is open and the lights are on. There she sits on her knees when he arrives. She sits bleeding with her face swollen. Jordan's fist swells and clenches to itself. He almost lost circulation in his small fat fingers. Suddenly Jordan begins to burn with passion. He's not sure where it came from or what it is. He felt a hatred so strong, but not for her husband but rather, for Meredith. He is just as hurt as she is; what she feels on the outside is what he looks like on the inside. Swollen, bleeding, beaten, torn. She's a lying, cheating whore. That's why she was beat. Her husband wasn't going to accept being fucked with so he popped her in the face a few times, broke her nose, and punched her around. Barely able to speak, she mutters the words out of her mouth as a subtle bit of humanity finally comes out in the form of a tear. Meredith doesn't cry, but now she can't hold it in any longer.

"I like it rough. You always knew that."

XIII. The Epidemic

Three bites is all it takes to get food poisoning. Actually, it takes a lot less to get someone sick, and in this case, the entire staff is sick. It's just one sick jackass who forgets to wash his hands. This is why food safety is important; it keeps the workers and the patrons safe from nasty bacteria that could possibly infect anyone. This is why people should call in when they get sick. It causes damage, a chain linking one person to another until everyone experiences the disgusting horrid feeling of bending over a toilet during a busy shift.

In other cases, illnesses can be caused by food that was left out overnight, or not cooked correctly, or even stored incorrectly. It's pretty obvious that you don't leave raw chicken meat in a warm environment for so many hours. But management will do anything and everything to keep their costs at an all-time low. Sometimes it works better if you don't know the truth.

When managers make more profit and actually gain new customers and new money over a quarter, they get a raise or a bonus. When managers keep their costs low while improving profits, they get a bonus. When food costs are lower, and they still get improved productivity and higher customer satisfaction and a higher profit, that's when the real bonuses happen. This would seem impossible, except that it isn't. Not if you keep food way past its expiration date. Not if you use that old food and serve it to your employees for their lunch breaks. That way a customer doesn't find out and get sick; the employees are a renewable resource constantly getting better, more efficient, honorable, and willing to put their lives on the line to make the money that the restaurant is actually making for them.

"Make sure your salad is out of the employee pot!" Dante exclaims. Just like a server in a big city, food is a horrible thing to waste.

So the day that Dante gets his bonus he gets to feed the entire restaurant staff. He makes it a point to say that he couldn't have done it without them.

"Here's to the hard work of the staff. Finish cleaning up and get yourself something to munch on."

The food is good. It's not made with the best of ingredients, but nobody has to know that. Nobody but the lovely manager. The servers come in one after another and get themselves some very high quality delicious three-week-past-expiration-date meat. The best kind. Laced with bonus checks.

It starts so simple. A small bite filled with the darkest bacteria covered with seasoning so strong it disguises the foul taste. Everyone enjoys it. All of the employees each bite in with a small sense of victory. Hard weeks came and went with no sense of it ending until this evening. Finally somebody is doing something nice for a change. Something really nice.

When the food enters the stomach it doesn't affect the victim immediately. It takes some time. Sooner or later, though, it gets through.

Finally after the night is over and everyone cleaned and fixed their sections and side work, all of the servers and kitchen staff go home.

It doesn't affect everyone the same. Sometimes it's a small discomfort—a minor ache in the stomach or some cramps. Some have to go to the restroom one or two times. Others don't have it so lucky. Vomiting, diarrhea, dehydration and pain. Pointless pain and suffering.

The next few days to follow, half the staff is out. Nobody figures out why because the restaurant can run on a shorter staff. If anything, it's over staffed.

The start of the day should be effortless. The people who are missing are the regular people that don't contribute to the actual efficiency of the business. Whether the weather is bad, and the storm is passing through the bowels, the rest of the world is still moving and going. People still need to feed themselves.

Managers always scoff at the idea of wanting or needing a day off. Whenever an employee calls in, it's incredibly informal and hard to get approval by anyone. The employees make a phone call sometimes minutes before their shift and say that they can't come in. "Did you get someone to cover your shift?" This is the first and only question that's always asked, and if the answer is no, then it is a write up. If some family emergency comes up, the business comes first. Unless a doctor's note is provided; then at any time an employer can fire an employee. This creates a huge issue because most of the workers here can't afford their own health care.

Labor laws don't really apply to the restaurant, and there rarely are any disputes within the business. Instead the workers just get impatient, pissed off, and leave to work elsewhere. They go to a place where the water is cleaner, the grass is greener, and the money comes quicker. The reality is it's all the same, just with a different skin. Like the saying goes, "blood is the same color in every race."

While the employees call in, they are too embarrassed to reveal their real problems, and with the management fully healthy and staffed, the small illness poses no real threat to the course of business. It's just upsetting and annoying to those who actually have to be there. Friday comes and people call in starting right at prep time. They begin to throw up from the night before. Then right before the shift starts a few more people call in. During lunch, Dante, the manager on duty, realizes he's short four servers, and the best part is that they all work doubles! Now he's scrambling to find replacements. He goes to the staff that's already there: Ethan, Jenn, Chelsea. He calls people at home and texts the numbers he has programmed in his phone: Jordan, Daniel, Stephanie. Finally, he hears back from Gez and Natalie. They wonder what he needs.

call me, need help tonight! I'll hook you up with good section.

Gez and Natalie are supposed to be off tonight and enjoy their Friday. They text back and forth separately before they both get back to Dante. They agree to come in if Dante hooks them up with more than good sections and food.

Dante, despite being a horrible human being, is well liked because he lets all the servers get away with whatever they want; he supplies them with recreational drugs like molly, pot, and drinks during the shift. Even though he's in his 30s and married, he plays best friend to all of the workers, especially the girls.

Dante reluctantly agrees to bring in some molly to Gez and Natalie who will pick up the shift. He also promises Jordan he'll supply him with beer and shots during and after work.

While Dante is trying to bribe young servers with drugs and alcohol, he realizes that one of his servers on the floor disappeared. Ethan is nowhere to be found during the middle of his lunch shift. Dante goes looking around for him in all parts of the restaurant. His section is losing money because the guests are just sitting around looking for someone to help. One of his tables is waiting for a check and the other has food but no drinks at the table. Dante wonders what the hell went wrong for all this to be happening during his shift. As he goes to the hostess stand to watch over Ethan's section, he receives a phone call. The caller wants to know if they can accommodate a party of 25 people. Dante is baffled. His heart starts to pound. He's scared to say yes and is also a little bit freaked the fuck out by the request. He is counting down the hours until Meredith gets here to help him out. He, with all his happy heart, says no to the customer. The customer wants to put up a fight but Dante has heard it all before.

"Yeah. Sorry. No, we just can't do it today. We don't have the staff and our room is already reserved for another party. Plus we can't put our tables together."

He is telling a complete lie. The tables at Chandler's have the capability of moving wherever the staff sees fit. With a morning rush, and tables already on wait and a short staff, there is nothing he can do to help that poor happy soul who wants to celebrate her best friend's baby shower. It doesn't really matter to him. All that matters is that he has to work 12 hours of hell.

He stands there watching guest after guest walk in, wondering how this is happening. Then he comes back on track and realizes that he is still searching for Ethan. He walks to the back, checking the walk-in cooler, the dry storage, the grill, the prep—nowhere. Finally he goes into the bathroom. Still doesn't see anyone there. He then takes a walk outside to see if by chance Ethan would be smoking. It was a stupid idea because Ethan doesn't smoke. As he comes in from the back door, he hears unpleasant and nasty sounds coming from the employee restroom. It's the sound of splattering liquid and muffled moans. He waits by the door until he hears a flush and then gets ready to face what is on the other side of the door. It's none other than Ethan, his new favorite server.

Ethan is pale and hunched over. Normally a good-looking, confident, skinny young man, but now looking like he's been starving himself. Dante doesn't want to ask but has to because of the nature of his job description. So he does. Disgusted.

"You okay?"

"Yeah. Must've been something I ate yesterday."

"Whoa...you're not going back out there are you?"

"I mean. I have to."

"Not if shit like that is coming out of you. *Hell* no. You're going to give me your cash out and go home."

"Don't worry about it. I'll make it. If I do it again, I'll tell you. Then I'll go home. I'm here to make some money. I got a car payment. I'll be good. Look."

Ethan pulls out some anti-nausea medicine out of his wallet.

"What's that?"

"I got sick a year ago. Really nasty stomach virus. Doctors gave me this. I keep it with me at all times. Too valuable to trash."

"Hmm... if I were you, I would've told someone it was something it's not and sold it."

"Well we all have to look after ourselves. Take care of my tables for another 10 minutes, okay? I'll be good."

186

"If I catch you again, you're going home!"

"I'll be good."

Ethan takes out a small aluminum cover and pokes a tiny white pill out of the back. He places it under his tongue and lets it dissolve. He has to get better if he's going to make his rent and have enough money to drive out to see his sister graduate next weekend.

Dante then takes himself to the front and delegates as necessary. At that moment he begins to wonder what is causing all of these call-ins. Seeing Ethan like that makes him think it all isn't just coincidental. He begins to wonder if it had to do with the feast they all served up the night before. Not wanting to take sole responsibility, he remembers another server calling in earlier this week. He can't remember the real reason why the server called in, but it's something he can use as insurance. He had a stomach bug. It wasn't completely gone, and he came in still. *Do viruses work like that?* he thinks to himself. Surely they do. He remembers reading somewhere that viruses can survive in the air and on surfaces for quite a long time. Or is that bacteria he's thinking of? It doesn't matter. People here don't look that far into things like he does. Constantly over-analysing every detail. So when Meredith finally shows up around 1:00, he knows to tell her that there is a bug going around.

Ethan is rationalizing his pain by thinking of seeing his family for the first time in a few months. *Too long.* He misses them. He doesn't know how or why it took this long to go back, but with constant bills, credit cards, and working to meet those payment due dates, he doesn't have time for much of anything. He's stuck working sick because he has to. There is no help with health bills here so a decision in his mind is working itself out. He could go home the next few days and pay his car bill late, or he could suck it up and make it out to Austin next weekend for a winter graduation. He knows he is in no condition to work the double he was supposed to, but he also is aware that if he makes it through this shift, he could come back and work a double on Sunday to make up the lost funds. He hates working Sundays but there isn't much of a choice. He could quit but that would stop him from leaving the area, and moving on to the next part of his life. He's determined to make it happen. He could work a normal job like all of his old classmates he keeps waiting on day after day, but who in an office would hire a person whose only experience is filling up salt shakers and ketchup bottles?

Dante is scrambling around. He wants to call Alden and Charlie to tell them what's going on, but Meredith stops him.

"You don't want them here. If it's just us we can keep it cool. We can keep it chill."

"You're right. More drinks for me too."

Dante decides he can run this shift himself. He does a quick sweep of the restaurant to make sure it's okay and clean. He talks to servers about their day and tries to recruit more workers for tonight and the rest of the weekend. He greets some tables to make sure that everything is good behind the chaos inside his own head. He does it to reassure himself not to panic and that this sort of thing happens all the time.

Despite the staff's case of explosive diarrhea, when he sees that the restaurant is still standing, he goes into the employee restroom and does a line of coke. He comes out and grabs a to-go cup and goes to his bag. He reaches for a silver scratched up flask. Inside it is a golden drink that is smooth and rich. He pours it into the cup almost half way. He discreetly walks to the soda gun at the bar and pours Diet Coke to fill up the rest. He puts a lid on it and a straw and takes four gulps.

"It's going to be a long weekend."

Occupied

The epitaph doesn't speak
To those who want to listen,
But rather to those who don't.

Once our time passes
Our work is more important
Than our lives that never happen,

Because we were too busy
Trying to make it.

XIV. To Go Box

Sometimes, people die for stupid fucking reasons. It was late afternoon, still light out, but getting darker. The sunset was something to remember in itself, coloring a canvas for something terrific to happen. It was unusually warm for the middle of winter but an arctic blast was scheduled to overcome the warmth that brought an outstanding amount of patrons to Dirty Murphy's BBQ.

Dirty Murphy's BBQ is located right off the interstate just north of the downtown area and neighbors Chandler's Casual Eatery. In comparison to the neighboring restaurants, Chandler's was the harder place to work at, and most of the servers working at Dirty Murphy's were those that left for greener pastures. Unlike Chandler's, Dirty Murphy's had more resources for a server to succeed: the food at Dirty Murphy's was priced higher, which meant for meatier tips, they had bussers, and designated food runners. They even had people to fill up water and tea around bigger sections. More money and half the work.

Dirty Murphy's is a place where they used the name and atmosphere to sell a story about how a family went from nothing to something. Throughout the restaurant, there are black and white grainy old film prints of the

191

family's history. It was featured on the show "Heavenly
Eats" for their famous meats and menu items that
featured all-you-can-eat ribs and sausage. It has always
been a famous tourist trap that locals found overrated.
Since they first opened as just Murphy's in 1915 as a
grocery store, they had time to grow their business. They
started offering sandwiches during lunch and then that
took business to a whole new level and they changed
their name. Now that they have commercialized and
grew to new heights in the restaurant industry they
became cheap and fake. The meats aren't even smoked
on location anymore, and in fact it all gets shipped from
the factory downtown. The margaritas don't even use
tequila as a base and instead, wine is substituted. The
food is as fake and as gaudy as the sign that can be seen
right at the entrance: "WORLD FAMOUS DIRTY
MURPHY'S BBQ."

Her name was Elizabeth, but she went by Liz. She
was a tiny girl. Petite. If you saw just her face, you'd
probably mistake her for a young boy because of her
short hair and androgynous chin. Liz hated living in
Texas. She hated the weather, the people, and the
obnoxious accent. But the weather was something she
found most peevish. She thought that seasons didn't exist
here, and with the day having a record high of 82
degrees, she was already in a bad mood. Liz was very

similar to every server that has ever worked. She was over the idea of making little money and doing the same thing every day while being tired, putting up with the customers that didn't know how to properly convey simple communications skills and mannerisms. Liz was disgusted with the state of restaurants in America. She displayed it in her walk as she stomped away in her little shoes.

While she hated her job, to Liz, it was a game to see how much money she could milk from the scum that came into eat their horrible excuse for grilled meats. Liz's customers were often satisfied with her fast service and orange personality; she was all tickles and lollipops to her customers—warm-hearted and very compassionate. She put on such a good act; it was almost impossible to know what was really going through her head.

Liz hasn't had a lot of problems with customers, that was, until that very warm night waiting on *those* two regulars.

Every employee thought the same about those particular regulars: disrespectful, rude, ugly, fat, and they tipped like shit. They left notes on their slips saying "good job," whilst only leaving less than 5% of the tab. They acted like everyone was their friend, greeting each employee by their first name. If only they didn't complain about various things throughout their visits. Maybe they were being ironic, but their behavior suggests they don't know the meaning of the word. They would finish their entire meal, and drink too much, but bitch about the food tasting bad and then come back the next week to eat the same thing. Basically they were looking for a free meal because, at least, they were smart enough to understand they could get away with it.

That night, Liz was their victim. Once their fat asses sat down, Liz didn't take long to greet them.

"Hello there, my name is Liz, I'll be taking care of—"

"Coke, she'll have water."

"—of you today... okay. Are we having a good day so far?"

"Better if I had a drink and food."

The man's words seemed lazy and he didn't make any eye contact. When the couple sat, the woman had trouble sitting down and holding her weight from crushing the chair below her, and the man couldn't fit both of his legs under the table and had one of them sticking out to the side. Liz knew that this table was going to be a nightmare, so she just smiled, and walked away. She went to the drink station to pour a Coke and a water and then walked back to the table smiling whispering to herself "fuck me."

She placed both drinks in front of their rightful owners and continued with the process. As soon as the drink hit the table, the couple grabbed them and drank.

"This ain't a Dr. Pepper. This is a Coke! I wanted a Dr. Pepper."

The woman already finished her water.

Liz, completely shocked, widened her eyes. She didn't believe it, but wasn't completely surprised. She forgot about the fact that southerners call every type of sweet caffeinated, carbonated soft drink a "coke."

"I'm sorry. I'll be right back with your Dr. Pepper."

"Get her a water, too. Bring two of each. We're thirsty."

"Sure thing." she said as her smile turned into something more menacing.

She came back and took their order. Both of them wanted the all-you-can-eat ribs option. *Of course*, she thought. By the time she took their menus, they were ready for another refill and complained about the weather.

Liz was busy, like always on a Friday, but having to keep up with their drinks was enough to make anyone get in the weeds. She had trouble keeping track of her other tables because all of her attention was directed to the couple with the bottomless pits. They requested refills five times before their food arrived in front of their chubby hands. It's a surprise that they could even properly hold on to the cups. She wondered where the hell the server assistants were. During this time, she didn't see a single kid to help with drinks—they were in the back playing with their "girlfriends."

When the food arrived, it wasn't up to their very high, impossible standards.

"What is this?"

"Sorry?"

"What the hell is this shit? Hardly any meat on the bones. Nothing to eat."

"Well, it's all you can eat. I can get you some more—some better—"

"Please do."

Liz had to go back and get some ribs that were just right. She had to inspect each single bone to make sure it was up to her own code she made up in her mind. When she brought them back there she was, the wife of the man with the bottomless stomach.

"This food is cold." She said in a tone as if her puppy was killed.

"I'll get you some fresh food." Liz said. "I'm completely sorry. This is just unacceptable at best." They couldn't tell, but Liz was being sardonic.

The man chimed in.

"This doesn't look like replacements, what, did you just reorder them and serve them back to me. Looks nothing like the show, looks nothing like the menu."

Of all the people that would know what the food would look like, they should know exactly what the food looks like, having eaten there every week for the past five months. The unusual thing about Liz being yelled at by her customers was her face and how rare it was. She normally was very animated showing her distaste for their attitudes, but instead that day, she was calm about it with a serene look on her eyes. The way they closed for a little bit like she was holding a sneeze, and then opened with a type of calm...a blank stare into space.

"We've been coming here for years, never have we had food this horrible, and the service since we walked in here has been slow, I mean c'mon," and then out of nowhere, his wife began to chime in, just on cue, "It's a real shame. This used to be our favorite place, but now it's just going downhill. I love visiting this place. We come to see family in town and our kids always take us here, but I don't know if we'll be coming back here again."

They continued to bitch and made sure they were loud enough for everyone to hear. *This place sucks, you suck, these prices are shit, you're shit, you suck, food sucks, everything sucks.* They just did not stop, and at that point Liz stood and stared when something unexpected came out of her mouth.

"I don't give a shit!" she said quietly. "Shut the fuck up." They continued on with their insults, calling her a little boy.

"Shut the fuck up!" Liz said loud enough for everyone to hear.

The couple, looking surprised at Liz's word choice yelled out what any normal person would yell at that moment. "Give me your manager!"

Liz composed herself and quietly whispered. "Get him your fucking self you fat piece of shit!" she said. She had one of those *what the fuck do you think you're doing* smiles when arguing. It was a creepy smile. She talked about his weight, and how they are the type of people destroying the working class of the nation with their ignorance. The lady started to talk back and Liz just shoved her hand in the woman's face pushing her back. The woman couldn't do anything because her hands were too short and stumpy to reach Liz. The man couldn't get up fast enough to do anything. They were powerless to defend themselves against a petite and quick waitress. The couple's faces were boiling and the man looked as if he was about to die, well, at that moment from a heart attack and not a bullet to his cholesterol infused heart.

The nosy customers all around stopped in silence but tried to continue eating.

The commotion reverberated around the dining room and finally caught the manager's attention. Liz, knowing that she wouldn't be able to defend herself, and knowing that the manager will take the customer's side, just walked away. As the manager looked at her, disappointed like a mother upset with their spoiled brat kids, he listened to the customer's concern and change of tone. The couple became polite, saying that they were the victims of a very rude Liz and concerned about the well being of Dirty Murphy's brand and her future as a server.

Liz didn't care what they thought. She wanted this moment to happen for such a long time. She wanted to tell off a customer, and go out in a blaze of glory.

She walked out, throwing her book in the middle of the dining room with the cash, tip slips, and everything else in it, hoping someone would take the restaurant's money. That didn't happen. In fact, everyone was wondering why this girl would be obnoxious enough to cause such a scene. She walked out and customers went back to their routines. In her car, she lit a cigarette and took her time smoking it. She opened a liquor bottle she was saving for later and drank a quarter of its contents as she does when she leaves her job. She blew out the smoke and saw that people were still eating and walking in. She thought about the uncharacteristically huge couple she just walked out on and pictured them laughing smiling at each other, getting what they wanted all along. More food to feed their fat faces. She thought of how they lived and how hard it must be to just get out of bed and brush their teeth. How difficult it is to be that big and take a bath, and then she got sick to her stomach thinking about how they look naked. She wondered how they have sex with that much fat covering their genitals, or even if they ever *had* sex. Rolls building up on one another creating hills of lard, slippery with grease and body odor.

Without hesitation she pulled out a gun. It rested in her car's glove box. Sitting in case someone would try to hurt her small body, a form of protection when she ventured out alone at night in the urban areas. She lit another cigarette with the one already lit in her mouth. She put the gun in her apron, got out of her car, and walked back into the restaurant.

BREAKING: A 22-year-old woman was gunned down by an off duty police officer at the local restaurant chain Dirty Murphy's BBQ after she opened fire on two customers, police said.

According to the statement made Sunday morning by officer Roch of the Riverside Police Department, the patrons at the restaurant began arguing and cursing at the employee. The manager was called to intervene and the employee walked away. Moments later, she came back and opened fire on the couple, then pointed the gun onto herself before she was fatally shot by Officer Roch.

The shooter's victims, Amy and George McGarry, were transported by ambulance to a nearby hospital where they remain in critical condition, a trauma doctor said. The restaurant stopped all operations and will be closed until further notice.

This story is developing, check back for updates.

TRACKING WINTER STORM: Temperatures drop more than 60 degrees in one hour.

XV. Rebirth

People still come to eat here after last week's incident. Dante calls it a new attraction. It's been a week since the shooting occurred, and it seems that nothing will stop the masses from visiting this small strip of restaurants where three people lost their lives. Chandler's sits next to the site and already it's a dark tourist attraction. Dante finds it hilarious as he drives up for his shift. This amuses him. Instead of protesters and reporters and yells and calls for gun reform, there is nothing but a brand new legend that the strip is haunted. Every restaurant on this block is filled with dying souls. Fuck, people still need to eat out, and while business could have been shut down at Chandler's, it's done the opposite effect.

Mary hates the foot traffic but is happy to know that she won't have to worry about buying formula for her expecting child. She is six months pregnant and wants the baby out of her already. Since day one she's held the toilet more than her husband who caused this.

She's excited for her second child in five years but doesn't recall her first pregnancy being riddled with so many emotions and nausea. She's typically a happy server and enjoys the company of most of her coworkers, but this pregnancy is just stressful and harder because it's so irratic and unpredictable. Will she have a good day or will she be running into the restroom to throw up her water? Going home isn't an option for her. She's strong-willed and wants to work until labor. She arrives at a crowded restaurant and they all want to know the same thing and go out of their way to ask the same questions about the prior week.

"Were you here when it happened?"

"Did you know them?"

"Are you cursed?"

Contrary to how bad humans as a collective race think the world is, several of those same people pay no attention to the general theater that is their local roots. There is no gratitude for a simple breath when it could be taken away by a pissed off server. None of it will change the person into something if it is not experienced firsthand. Mary worries about her unborn child, her future, and her own well-being. She cares about everything that includes all that she can't control. She worries about how a certain election turned out and what it might mean to be a woman and a minority woman at that. The ridicule that would possibly greet her walking in the store, and the sexism and racism that will tear her down.

It wasn't until after the gunshots that she truly knew how to not worry about the proverbial bomb going off in her face. Nobody is going to treat her kids like low class immigrants. If it does happen, she will deal with it, until it does, she won't worry about anything.

Mary's customers don't worry about this. Her tables worry about getting food, not about some theoretical scenario that exists only in her mind. They don't care about the people who were killed next door. They worry if their steak is cooked properly. They are more worried about their chicken being cooked right than they are about the guy who raped a 17-year-old here. They are more concerned about their check balance and happy hour price than about a young man getting his heart broken and ripped.

They don't care about the past, or what happened or the story behind the server, just their food, drinks, and company.

And that's okay. Mary understands this.

Mary walks straight, sits down in a corner table hidden in the far back of the restaurant, and waits for her trainee to show. This section is closed for the day. She places her purse down and sends a message to her husband.

HOW IS YOUR DAY? DOIN FINE...MADE IT TO WORK...TRAINING TODAY SO WON'T BE ABLE TO RESPOND. CALL YOU WHEN I'M OFF. LOVE YOU

She remembers a table she had when she started here four years ago. Her first week as a server dealing with a table that wanted a medium rare steak but instead got served a well-done steak. It's shit because fuck if that customer didn't deserve that perfectly cooked steak after a long day. The one thing they were looking forward to. She got yelled at by the customers, the cooks, and the manager at the time. She smiled, scoffed and rolled her eyes. She looked down and took a long deep breath thinking about all the times someone was pissed off here.

She's still here. She's still doing better now in spite of the numerous customer complaints over the years. She looks ahead now thinking that tomorrow will be better because she makes more people smile than sneer. It's better for her, better for the child inside her, and better to be thankful. She thinks everyone should work this job at least once for a month. She thinks that could save the world a lot of heartache.

The child inside will be thankful for someone like her in their life, and Mary will teach this child that love and empathy is worth waking up and going to a shitty job.

Don't be anyone else. She thinks as her trainee walks in.

Don't be anyone else.

She looks at this fresh young girl, thinking that she'll be here only for a moment. It'll pass before management does its turnover. This place is just a bus stop to a final destination.

"Hey, I'm Mary. Work in a restaurant before?"

"No, actually."

"Customer service?"

"It's my first job."

Oh sweet innocence and naivety. She thinks that this girl is going to be fucked up after leaving this place.

"Don't worry about it. It's pretty easy but it does take time. You can make some good money doin' it. If you do it right. Really, it's what you make of it. It's a job. Just be real with your customers and your coworkers and you'll be good. Just be you."

Just be fuckin' you. Don't be anyone else.

"How long have you been here?" she asks, completely unaware of the road ahead. Unaware of the trips she'll take and hearts she'll break. The weight she will gain and lose, the friendships she'll make, or won't make and the shit she'll learn.

The lives she'll see in front of her eating away their pleasures, putting it all in, stuffing themselves with their own well being. Oblivious to the fact that maybe she'll find love in this cold world in one of those workers who fills the same ice pit as she does. She may get hurt, she may not, but it's up to her on how she takes the pain and becomes something greater and something more than she could ever think of herself to be. To be pushed to deal with the people of the world in a way she didn't think of. Whether she's here, or working at another restaurant, she will both love to the heights of heaven and hate through the pits of hell. Here. This is where she will grow. Like Mary, she will become services, she will become humility, pride, jealousy, and compassion. Avarice, generosity, She isn't the job, the job is her. She isn't here to live, she is here to make a living—to pay her bills, to be appreciated, to be adored, to be fucked, to be fucked over.

"Too long."

Mary responds as she tires and the baby kicks. A Braxton Hicks contraction takes over her body and the baby will soon be here to elevate her away to a mother's life.

"Are you okay?" The trainee asks.

"It's just a contraction—I get them a lot now. It must be getting smaller in there. He's ready to come out to see the world."

ACKNOWLEDGMENTS

To you... yes you... right there... you're the best person ever and I love you! Thanks for your support and reading this book!

A special thank you to Ariel, the love of my life, for putting up with my random ramblings that make no sense to the context of them being delivered. Thank you to my mother for supporting me and my father who always told me to never stop writing and to always hold on to it. Thank you to my siblings for helping me through the hard times of my life.

Thank you to all the workers out there who are putting forth their best efforts in a trying time like this.

Thank you Ashley, my editor, who agreed to take on this project and did not know what she was getting herself into.

Thank you to my best friend, Mason, who stayed with me for 22 years and worked the industry with me.

This book is also dedicated to my two very young children, and all eight of my nieces and nephews.

About the Author

Joseph Anzaldua earned a B.A. in English Literature from the University of North Texas. This is his debut Novel. Joseph is a crazy man who wrote a book and works crazy jobs. He has two kids, a wife, two cats, and lives somewhere in Texas.

Follow him @janzimages on twitter and instagram.

Made in the USA
Columbia, SC
12 July 2022